Mistress
of the
Moor

Mistress
of the
Moor

ABIGAIL CLEMENTS

A FAWCETT GOLD MEDAL BOOK

Fawcett Publications, Inc., Greenwich, Conn.

MISTRESS OF THE MOOR

Printed in the United States of America

March 1974

Chapter One

My Dear Emma,

I want to ask a great favor of you. Though I have not seen you since the tragic events of two years ago when your dear Aunt was lost to us in that sad and horrible manner, I remember you so well as a child here at Goathlands. You were always my favorite niece and I watched with great happiness as you grew up into a charming and beautiful lady. I sometimes wondered if you would not have been happier had you been a boy. There was always a streak of independence in you, one which I doubt if even my brother could have curbed, and it came as no surprise to me when, after your father was lost in South Africa, you decided to go to London and earn your own living.

My dear, that was eight years ago and times have changed. We are now almost through the first decade of the twentieth century, the old Queen has gone and with her a great many of the prejudices that epitomized her reign. There are no raised eyebrows here in Goathlands when I tell people that my favorite niece is a "lady typewriter" in London; there is rather a sense of admiration.

I always felt that you needed to be needed and that if this circumstance was lacking you would never be interested in anything. Dear Emma, I want to put that opinion to the test, for I need you now.

I have two positions vacant here, both of which can be filled by only one person. Because of the nature of

*my present research, these positions can only go to a
person in whom I have complete and absolute trust. Details I cannot give you until I know for certain that you
will accept, but broadly speaking, one post would be
that of hostess at Goathlands while the other, which in
my opinion is the one which will require the greatest
trust and may provide the greatest temptations, is that
of confidential lady typewriter to myself.*

*I am sorry that at this time it is impossible for me to
give you any further details, but I am sure you will understand the urgency when I say that a reply by return
of post is essential.*

*If you accept this offer, rather odd-sounding I must
admit, I would like you to leave London on the Flying
Scotsman on Friday. You would arrive in York in time
to catch the four P.M. train to Malton.*

*A carriage will be waiting for you at the station to
drive you to Goathlands. There I shall be waiting for
you and there, when we meet, you will understand why
it would be impossible for me to drive to the station myself.*

*If, and I hope that this will not be the case, you
should decide that you cannot accept for any reason
whatsoever, then I must ask you to please destroy this
letter and do not reply.*

*There is little more that I can say except to reiterate
that which I said earlier. I need you. How true this is
will be revealed to you but slowly, but in considering
this, do remember that the one thing I need more than
anything is your complete and absolute trust.*

I await your reply and pray that it comes,

> *Always your loving Uncle,*
> *Joshua.*

The letter had arrived at nine o'clock in the morning. I
read it for the fifth or sixth time. Of course I remembered

Uncle Joshua; I remembered him well. A jolly, rather tubby man with a great red smiling face and a huge brow, so shiny that you might almost have used it for a vanity mirror. Really, he looked more like a Dales farmer than Sir Joshua Waldron, Bart., Master of Goathlands.

There was nothing of the aristocrat about Uncle Josh. He loved tinkering; anything mechanical was a matter of great joy to him. I believe that he owned no less than three of those horrid, smelly horseless carriages, two of which he had built himself.

His wife, my dear Aunt Hester, had died tragically and horribly two years ago when the fire gutted the west wing and central hall of Goathlands. I was in Paris at the time, typewriting at the British Consulate, and did not hear of these terrifying happenings until my return to London several months later. Of course I wrote immediately to express my sympathy, but the reply came, not from Uncle Joshua, but from his son, Cousin Henry. He advised me against visiting Goathlands, as Uncle Josh was under medical care and the doctors advised against visitors. I tried to contact my uncle on two further occasions, but both replies were from Cousin Henry, who continued to discourage me from visiting Goathlands. After that I gave up, and over the next eighteen months there was silence. Now this letter!

The question I had to answer was simple. Should I decide here and now that I should go to Goathlands, or should I destroy the letter and forget that it had ever been written?

If I decided to accept Uncle Joshua's proposition there would be no obstacle to my instant departure from London. I was not in any form of regular employment; I was typing play scripts for theatrical producers, including one script, if you will forgive the pride, for no less a person than Sir Herbert Beerbohm Tree. This I could quite easily finish in the three days before Friday. The trouble was that Uncle Joshua's letter said absolutely nothing except to express his almost desperate desire for me to come to Goathlands.

I loved Goathlands; I was born there, and the childhood memories of that dear spot were still very close to my heart. I am sure that it was this fact more than any other which caused me to make my decision and to reply to Uncle Joshua with what must have been one of the shortest letters ever written. It ran:

Dear Uncle Josh,
  Send your carriage to Malton, I shall be there.

Love,
Emma.

It was twenty minutes to ten on the morning of Friday, the ninth of October, 1909, when the porter put my trunk into the luggage van. I breathed deeply the smell of that wonderful aromatic mixture of steam and coal smoke and looked at the massive locomotives, hissing and wheezing as they waited for the guiding hands of their drivers to send them hurtling along their metal ways to all the corners of the country. I was filled with childhood memories of trains and stations: going home from school, home to Goathlands. I felt like a child again as I settled comfortably into a corner seat in a "Ladies Only" compartment, peering at the station clock while the seconds ticked away —until the upright minute hand signaled the Flying Scotsman away on the start of its four-hundred-mile journey north through York, Newcastle, and on to Edinburgh. The hand jumped the last half-minute. It was ten o'clock. With a great clanking and hissing, the giant engine backed its fourteen coaches together and then drew them apart to the full stretch of their couplings. Then the train smoothly and almost silently glided toward the first of the long tunnels which lie to the north of Kings Cross Station.

I'm going home! I'm going home! I'm going home! As the speed of the man-made monster increased, the wheels pounded the rhythm of those words faster and faster into my ears. Goathlands was home, and it always would be, even though it was eight years since I had been there. On my last day at Goathlands, I had wept in the village chapel while they held a memorial service for my dear father, killed in action near Kimberley. Though the following day I had left Goathlands, resolving never to return, I knew now, as deep in my heart I always had known, that Goath-lands was home. The clay of the North Yorkshire moors on which it stood was the clay which had formed me. The windswept gorse and the angry North Sea, the golden but-tercups of spring, the song of the lark, and the deep soft snow of the winter were all part of me. The fishermen of Whitby and Scarborough, the farmers of the Yorkshire moors and dales who used to explain to a little girl the wonders of their crafts, the smell of horses at the racing stables near Malton, the scent of wildflowers in Troutdale, York hams hanging from the beams in the pantry, living coal and log fires flickering and crackling in the fireplaces —I remembered them all. I wondered how many of the people there would remember Emma, a little girl with pink ribbons in her hair and freckles which she tried to rub off with her school eraser. Then there was Honey, my Welsh pony. He was the color of his name, with a long white tail and mane and dun-colored legs which always made him look as if he had been standing up to his knees in mud all day. People used to call him "the rocking-horse pony." He should still be there; he would be fifteen now. Would Honeybunch remember me, come trotting across his field to greet me, and munch the apple that I always carried for him while I whispered all my secrets in his dear fuzzy ear? Next to Uncle Josh, I think I wanted to see Honey again more than anyone.

I'm going home! I'm going home! The words pounded

in my ears as the wheels clattered over the gaps in the rails and we raced through the flat expanse of Lincolnshire. I was going home to Uncle Josh, Honey, and, of course, Cousin Henry. I wondered about Henry; he and I had never been close. He was older than I and I remembered him as a tall, handsome youth who had very little time for a female cousin five years his junior. When I thought about Henry I realized that I did not really know him at all; I never had. My grandfather, the first baronet, had left the estate and all of the income in trust to Uncle Joshua, on whose death the house and title would of course go to Henry. But my grandfather's not-inconsiderable fortune was to be divided into three parts, one part going to Henry and the other two going to myself as the only other grand-child. It was a somewhat unusual and controversial will in an age when younger sons usually got nothing more than a token income and women received nothing apart from the family efforts to arrange a good match. I felt, rightly or wrongly I did not know, that Henry had always resented this, in spite of the known fact that at Uncle Joshua's insti-gation, the will had been drawn up in those terms.

For myself, it would have been less than honest to sug-gest that the prospect of a very comfortable and indepen-dent life gave me no satisfaction. But this did not really matter so very much. After all, I was capable of earning my own living. I had proved it over the last eight years. Now, I had reached a stage when, at twenty-six, wealth had but a limited appeal to me, and marriage seemed a rapidly disappearing vision.

We were through Doncaster, and my reverie was inter-rupted by the sight of the broad acres of my native York-shire. The names on the little wayside stations became more and more familiar. As we passed through Bishops-thorpe, I rose from my seat and got my hand luggage down from the rack, realizing for the first time that I was hungry. All the thoughts which had raced through my mind as we sped northward, through the beautiful autumn English countryside, had made me forget all about food. But no matter. Some tea and a sandwich at the Station Hotel in York would be a pleasant way of passing the hour I had to wait for my connection to Malton.

It was raining in Malton when the train pulled into the little station, and the wind was getting up. As I reached the door of my compartment, a familiar figure came trotting along beside it until the train lurched and was still. He flung the door open.

"Little Miss Emma," said Ormerod, a huge smile creasing his gnarled features into another million wrinkles. "Welcome home."

This huge man, well over six feet tall, his massive frame completely filling the door of the compartment, must by now have been approaching his sixtieth year. I had always loved Ormerod—dear, big, sweet, gentle Ormerod. He was my uncle's head groom and coachman when I was a child. It was he who taught me how to ride, how to handle a pair of hackneys, and where to find a plover's nest. Most important of all, it was he who found Honey for me. "The prettiest little yearling I ever did see, and he'll be a good 'un," was how he described him.

I was delighted to see Ormerod. I must confess I had been just a little apprehensive at the prospect of being met by my rather aloof cousin Henry. When Ormerod said, "Welcome home," I knew that home I was. I felt home. I put my hand into his great calloused paw, which could have bent an iron bar as easily as I could have snapped a twig, and he gently helped me to alight into the wonderful, clean, refreshing Yorkshire rain. I told him, and I meant it, how nice it was that he should be the one to meet me. His face creased into another huge smile, and he said, "When I heard that thou was coming home, I did try to put it into Sir Joshua's mind that I should be the one to meet thee. But come now, let's get thee into the waiting room so that I can get thee ready for the ride home."

"You haven't brought saddle horses?" I said, surprised and apprehensive. It was twenty miles to Howl Moor, where Goathlands stood.

"Nay, lass," he replied. "Thou could not be more wrong. I've got one of Sir Joshua's horseless carriages. But there's no coach roof and it's going to be a bit wet, so I've brought thee a motoring coat, sou'wester, and goggles. Come now, Miss Emma, we'll get thee wrapped up and we'll be off."

I am only five feet, and the coat must have been made for a tall man, for when I put it on it lay in concertinalike folds around my feet. Ormerod laughed and told me that it was probably a good thing, as it would certainly keep me drier than one which had been fashioned to fit me.

Outside the station yard, the motor car had already attracted the attention of a crowd of small urchins, but they rapidly dispersed under the lash of Ormerod's tongue.

"Begging thy pardon, Miss Emma, but that kind don't understand any other language."

I smiled and assured him that I was not shocked, as indeed I was not, having heard much worse language in the glittering salons of London society.

The porter came out of the station with my luggage. I told him to put it on the back seat, as I had no intention of being separated from Ormerod during the journey home. There was so much I wanted to ask him, so much that I wanted to know before we arrived at Goathlands.

Alas for my desire for information. Ormerod sat me in the passenger seat and wrapped me in a great rug, and then he went to the front of the machine, spat on his hands, and proceeded to wind the starting handle so fiercely that for the life of me I feared that the motor car would turn over. There were one or two loud explosions before the engine finally burst into life. What a rattling and a clanking it was. It caused a couple of horses, standing in their shafts on the cab rank, to shy so violently that the poor creatures lost a good proportion of the feed from their nosebags. Once the engine had started, any attempt at conversation would have been futile. So we rattled and snorted out of Malton toward Pickering and the north and away across the moors toward Goathlands.

Once or twice during the journey I smiled at Ormerod, though I don't think he noticed me. He sat there, a study in grim concentration, gripping the wheel and occasionally adjusting one of the countless little levers with which the carriage was equipped. We traveled at great speed. I learned later that on occasions we exceeded thirty miles to the hour, a truly great speed. And I quite believe it, for it was certainly less than an hour after leaving Malton that I caught my first glimpse of Goathlands, rising stark and massive from the moorland waste which surrounded it. The house stood on the edge of Howl Moor, one of a group of smaller areas which together comprised Goathlands Moors.

I don't know what I expected. After the fire, I was sure that Goathlands would have been remodeled, that it would not be the Goathlands that I remembered. But there it was, the same mass of contrasts that I had loved so much as a child. The house was stark but solid, of cold gray stone, but not without a suggestion of the warmth inside. The lights shone pale in the windows as they combated the gathering gloom. Goathlands was grim but honest. It did not give friendship easily, and yet it reached out across the moors to embrace those whom it loved. No, it had not changed; it was still home.

The motor car clattered up the drive and snorted to a halt outside the great front door, which had been hewn from old English oak two centuries earlier. Ormerod helped me down from my seat.

"Thou art to go straight in, Miss Emma. Thou will find Sir Joshua in the library."

We went into the oak-paneled hall, which was half-obscured by the shadows cast by the flickering gas jets as they strove to take over from the fast fading day. I removed my motoring coat and the sou'wester and handed them to Ormerod.

"Ormerod, can you tell me. . . ." I ventured.

"No, miss, it's better that thou go straight in." I suggested that it might be more polite if I were to freshen up first, but he would have none of it. He took the coat and the sou'wester and left me standing before the library door. I tapped lightly.

"Come."

I opened the door and entered the room. At the far end was a log fire flickering in the grate. This was flanked by two wing chairs, both of which were turned three-quarters toward the fire. On the arm of the right-hand chair, I could see a hand.

"Uncle Josh?"

"Emma, my dear, I want you to stay where you are for a moment. No, don't come closer until I tell you." I had taken a pace towards him. "Emma, I wish that I could spare you this, but I cannot, and within the next thirty seconds you are going to receive a shock. Now please understand that I don't mind whatever your reaction may be. You may scream, faint, or display any other expression of disgust or alarm. This is something which face you must, for you are going to have to live with it for as long as you are here at Goathlands. Do you understand?"

"Not really, Uncle," I replied hesitantly. "But I shall try to."

"That will be sufficient for the moment. Now I want you to walk straight over to the fire, turn, and face me. And Emma, don't be too afraid of what you will see."

Slowly, nervously, I walked to the fireplace and gripped the mantelpiece with my hands.

"Look, Emma, look!"

It was a command. I took a deep breath and turned.

For the first time in my life, I fainted.

Chapter Two

"WELCOME HOME, COUSIN."

Henry was bending over me, his handsome face looking positively boyish in the firelight. I tensed in the chair in which I was sitting and stared toward the one which had been occupied by Uncle Joshua.

"Don't worry, Emma, he's gone." Henry smiled sympathetically. "He won't come back until you are ready. Here, drink this. Come now, it is purely medicinal."

He handed me a glass of brandy, pressing it into my hand. "Go on now, you need it."

I sipped the brandy and tried to collect my thoughts. Was it true? Was that mass of purple scar tissue really my father's brother? In the fleeting glimpse I had had, I had been unable to take in any details but it was horrible . . . horrible.

"Hello, Henry." I tried to smile. "Did I . . . was it really Uncle Josh?"

"Oh yes, it was him, all right."

"But nobody told me. I never knew. When, how did it happen?"

"In the fire. He's been like that for two years. For

weeks after it happened we just waited for him to die, but
he didn't. He refused to. Day after day, only his will stood
between him and the grave, and when he finally recovered
sufficiently to look at himself in a mirror, it was only his
will that kept him from going mad. He has never been out-
of-doors since, and he swears that no one outside of his
family will ever look upon his face for as long as he lives."

I did not reply. Henry seemed to be very understanding;
he stood in silence while I sipped my brandy. I glanced at
his face, which was devoid of any expression. When he
caught my eye, a faint smile flickered across his lips. Was
he laughing at me? Was it a smile of sympathetic friendship? Or was he mocking me for my squeamishness? I did
not know, but I had to prove myself. "Henry," I said, "ask
him to come back."

"Are you sure?" he queried.

"Quite sure," I replied. "It was unkind of me to lose
control as I did. I must see him right away. Now."

"Very well, if you insist." His smile strengthened. Was
it sardonic? How I wished I could answer that.

"Are you trying to prove something?" he asked. "This
can wait till morning, you know. He will quite understand."

"Yes, Henry, I am trying to prove something, and it
cannot wait till morning. It must be now."

"Whatever you wish," said Henry, again with that enigmatic smile, and he was gone.

I was alone in the library; it was probably the room that
I knew least in the whole house. In Grandfather's day it
had been his inner sanctum, into which children did not
intrude. I had never felt really comfortable in the library
and now. . . . The thing I had seen, could that really be my
dear Uncle Joshua? Now I was committed to facing him
again. I knew that I was right in insisting that it had to be
now. For if I did not see him then, I knew that nothing in

the wide world would persuade me to spend a single night in that house.

The fleeting glimpse I had had of my uncle had left no clear impression in my mind's eye. I knew only that he looked horrible, but, knowing that, I felt that I should now be able to accept the physical fact and see beneath the surface to the kindly, jolly man I used to know. My thoughts were interrupted by a tap on the door.

"Come in," I said, thinking that it was rather strange of Henry to knock. But it was not Henry who answered my summons; it was a woman I had never seen before. She was tall and thin. Her features were flat, almost oriental; she had small eyes set wide apart, thin lips, and black hair drawn severely back from her forehead into a bun at the nape of her neck. She was wearing a black satin gown which had starched lace cuffs and a Tudor ruff. The severity of her dress was relieved by a single cameo on her bosom which I immediately recognized as having belonged to my aunt. She was dressed rather as one would expect a housekeeper to dress, and though Goathlands was large, it had never to my knowledge boasted a housekeeper.

"Miss Waldron?" In contrast to her severe appearance, her voice was low and soft, as well as being extremely cultured. "I am Susan Harrison. Henry told me that you wanted to see Sir Joshua immediately. If you would care to accompany me, I will take you to him."

Who was she? She had referred to Cousin Henry by his first name; this alone indicated that she was more than a servant. I resolved to ask her straight out. It was somewhat forward of me, no doubt, but I had no desire to be plagued by more mysteries.

"Miss Harrison?" I questioned. "It is 'Miss,' is it not?" The woman nodded, smiling a little. I continued, "May I be so presumptuous as to inquire as to your position in this house? I hope I do not offend by asking you, but I

have been away for some years and I should like to find
out as quickly as possible who people are. You're not a
guest, are you?" I had couched my rather rude question in
the most inoffensive terms that I could think of on the spur
of the moment.

She remained smiling faintly as I spoke. "No," she replied. "I am not a guest. I am a doctor." Observing my
puzzled expression, she added, "I am a doctor of medicine. I live at Goathlands and I attend Sir Joshua, as well,
of course, as anyone else in the house who should need my
services. You seem surprised."

I was completely taken aback. I had of course heard
that there were such persons as lady doctors. There must
have been a dozen or more throughout the country, but I
had never met one, nor had I ever expected to meet one.
And certainly not a lady doctor who was attending a male
patient, and that no other than my uncle.

"I think we had better go and see Sir Joshua now," she
continued. "He is expecting you, and he retires early.
Anyhow, you and I can talk after dinner. Will you come
with me now, please?"

"Yes, of course, Miss . . . er . . . Doctor," I murmured,
feeling somewhat embarrassed at granting that title to another woman.

As we walked through the corridors toward the rebuilt
west wing, I discovered that Uncle Josh had had an apart-
ment constructed there for his own use, and that he sel-
dom ventured beyond it. Dr. Harrison informed me that
the only other room in the house which he ever visited was
the library, and that only when he wanted some text which
was not easily explainable to her.

When we reached the door of his sitting room, she
stopped and turned to me. Her tone had lost its softness
and her voice had become quite firm, almost hard in fact.
"Remember," she said, "he is not a pretty sight, but this is
something you are going to live with. I don't want him

hurt by any display of emotion." And then, almost echoing my own thoughts, she said, "The kindest thing you can do is to ignore his disfigurement and treat him just as you would if he looked the same as when last you saw him."

There was great authority in her voice, and I felt a little afraid of her. However, I felt that this was probably a good thing, since it made me feel much less afraid of what I was about to see.

"I'll be all right," I said.

"Good," she replied. "He will ring if I should be needed. You can go in now." And with that she was gone. She didn't seem to walk away; she just turned on her heel and disappeared in the shadows of the corridor where we stood.

I was now alone and on the threshold of looking again upon that fearsome mass of scar tissue which had been my beloved uncle. For a moment, panic welled within me. I wanted to turn and fly, to find Ormerod and beg him to take me away from Goathlands for good. But the feeling was momentary. What kind of a person was I, to place so high a value on physical beauty? The man I was going to see *was* Uncle Joshua, the same Uncle Josh who used to piggy-back me around the nursery, who used to press an illegal piece of chocolate into my hand when I had already had my ration for the day. What sort of a person was I, to let a mere physical deformity turn me from one I had always loved?

I raised my hand to tap upon the door, but before it could fall, a voice from within the room interrupted me.

"Emma, don't run away; please come in. I did not lie when I said that I needed you."

I took a deep breath and turned the doorknob. The glass felt cold to the touch, for my hands were very hot. I walked into the room.

He was standing with his back to the fire as I entered. I held my head high and looked straight at him. I swallowed and tried hard to smile, all the time feeling the tears welling in my eyes. I ran my tongue over my dry lips and opened my mouth to greet him, but no word came.

How can I describe him? The left side of his face was almost as it had been, but the right side was completely covered with mottled purple scars. His right ear had gone completely, and his poor right eye stared sightlessly from a jagged hole. The right side of his scalp was completely bald, made all the more revolting by the tufts of hair still remaining on his good side. I understood now that Henry had not been exaggerating when he suggested that a weaker man might have gone mad at the first sight of what had once been his face.

"Take a good look, Emma, for in this I can spare you nothing." Only the left side of his mouth moved as he spoke. "But remember, no pity. Pity is a weak emotion, and it is strength that I need from you."

"Yes, Uncle Josh," I answered weakly.

"Welcome home, my dear," he said, and tried to smile a greeting. "Come and sit down. I am not going to ask you to stay for more than a moment. I do know that I am not a very handsome sight, and I am also aware that our first meeting was a great shock to you. Would you care to join me in a glass of sherry?" And as I started to protest, he said, "You will find two glasses already poured on that table over there; forgive me, I'm sorry."

He had indicated the table in question with his right hand, which until now, had been behind his back. There was no hand but just a smooth stump where the hand had once been.

"That's all right, Uncle," I replied, feeling my self-control creeping back. "And I should love to drink a glass of sherry with you."

"Good girl," he said, and indicated his handless arm. "This is, of course, the reason that I must have someone to do my writing for me. Thank you," he said as I handed him the glass. "We have only a few minutes before the dressing-gong, and I am sure you must be hungry after your journey."

"If you don't mind, I would rather not go down to dinner tonight. It has been a very exhausting day, and I should like to retire early. Perhaps a sandwich and a glass of warm milk in my room?" I did not of course tell him that the shock of seeing him in his present condition had entirely sapped any reserves of energy I might have possessed.

"Just as you wish, my dear." Almost as though he had read my thoughts, he added, "And seeing me has made the thought of polite table talk an embarrassment, eh?"

For a few moments we sipped our sherry in silence. I got the feeling that Uncle Joshua wanted me to use this first meeting merely to accustom myself to his appearance. This opinion was confirmed when after a long moment of silence he said, "Emma, I am not going to talk to you tonight. We shall meet again at ten-thirty tomorrow morning when we can discuss at length what I need of you. I am sure that you would prefer that we do it that way."

"Whatever you say, Uncle Josh," I replied. The conflict between fatigue and curiosity was quite overwhelming, but I was quite sure that he was right. In my heart I welcomed his suggestion.

"I shall arrange for Barton to take milk and sandwiches to your rooms. By the way, have you seen them yet?"

"No, Uncle. Shall I not be going back to my old room?" I asked.

"You are to have your grandmother's bedroom and sitting room in the east wing. I think you will be quite at home there. I arranged for some of your own furniture to be moved in to make it more familiar."

"That was very kind and thoughtful," I replied. "But

you need not have bothered. My old room would have been perfectly satisfactory. I was very fond of it, you know."

"Emma, for as long as you care to stay here, I want you to regard yourself as mistress of Goathlands. That is why you are to occupy those rooms. As far as the house is concerned, you will have an entirely free hand, and. . . . But here I am chattering away, and unless I am mistaken, that is the dressing-gong I hear. Would you be so kind as to ring?"

I pulled the tapestry bell pull, which was close to my left hand. Within a moment, Dr. Harrison came into the room.

"Emma has decided not to dine tonight and is going to her rooms now. Would you tell Barton to take warm milk and sandwiches up before he serves dinner?"

"Of course," replied Dr. Harrison. "Are you ready now, Miss Waldron?" I looked at Uncle Josh, who nodded faintly. I rose, feeling a little uncomfortable. Had the doctor not been present I think I might have had the courage to kiss his poor scarred brow. On the other hand, her presence saved me from making a gesture which may have been an embarrassment to both of us.

"Doctor," I said, "I know the way very well. I am sure that I can find my grandmother's room. There is really no need for you to bother." I smiled at her, trying not to make it sound like a snub. In this I fear I failed, but I really did want to be alone and I found the lady doctor a strangely dominant person.

"Just as you wish, Miss Waldron," she replied, with no hint of her feelings in the soft tones of her voice.

"Good night, uncle," I said. "Ten-thirty?" He nodded, and I left the room.

Goathlands is a substantial, though not an enormous, house. I walked slowly along the corridors and through the hall, up the main staircase and onto the second floor of the east wing, which housed my grandparents' apartments. I remembered my grandmother's rooms well; the entrance to them was through the second door along the main corridor. As a child I had always regarded it as a great treat to take afternoon tea with her in her sitting room. As I entered, I could almost see her surrounded by the silver tea service, the cucumber sandwiches, and the little cakes covered with pink icing with a cherry in the center of each one.

I went through into the bedroom. Here an old and familiar sight met my gaze, for lying on the covers, his head on the pillow, was my dear Nana. Nana was my teddy bear; my father had given him to me on my third birthday. He was much bigger than I was at the time, and he was soft and cuddly and I loved him. How kind of someone to remember this and put him there.

The lights were on, and a wave of nostalgia crept over me as I looked at the familiar flowered wallpaper, the chintzes and the curtains all a mass of pink roses, the dressing table wearing its pretty rosebud farthingale, and grandmama's great four-poster bed with its lace hangings and scalloped baldachino. In the sitting room, the rosewood table, the regency chairs, and the lovely, soft, comfortable chesterfield all conjured up memories of a wonderfully happy childhood.

I started fantasizing. I could hear grandmama's voice again as she patted the chesterfield and bade me sit beside her. I remembered the soft tread of my nanny's feet as she came to collect me and return me to the nursery at the end of what was always one of the happiest hours of the day. Grandmama played a very vital part in my childhood. I never knew my mother, since she died when I was born, but no one could have ever been more of a mother to me than my darling grandmama.

There was a tap on the door of the sitting room, and Barton came in with my tray. Here was another old friend,

another link with the past. As a young man he had entered
service with my grandfather and had gone to the Boer War
as my father's batman. After my father was killed, Barton
had returned to Goathlands, where now he was Uncle
Joshua's butler. He greeted me warmly, and I responded in
like manner. Then I asked him whether the water was hot,
as I wished to take a bath after my journey.

"Oh, yes, Miss Emma," he replied. "You'll never go
short of hot water here. And by the way, Miss, Sir Joshua
has ordered me to engage a personal maid for you. Would
you like me to send her up so you can meet her?"

I did not want to appear unkind, but I really was tired.
"If you don't mind, I think I shall bathe and go straight to
bed," I replied.

"Very well, Miss Emma," said Barton. "I will tell her to
put the warming pan into the bed and to bank up the fire
while you are in the bath. Are there any further instructions?"

"I would like early morning tea at eight o'clock, and the
maid . . . what is her name, by the way?"

"Leticia, miss, though everyone calls her Letty."

"Then I shall follow custom and also call her Letty.
Would you tell Letty that should I miss her tonight, I shall
be pleased to make her acquaintance when she brings my
tea in tomorrow morning."

"Very good, Miss Emma." Barton paused.

"Was there something else?" I inquired.

"Just that I should like to say, on behalf of all of us
below stairs, how nice it is to see you back at Goathlands,
miss. Good night, miss, and I shall inform Mr. Henry that
you will not be down to dinner."

"Thank you," I replied. "Good night, Barton."

My bathroom led directly off the bedroom. As I lay in
the deep, hot water, letting it dissolve away all the travel
stiffness and thinking how nice it was to be home again, I
could hear the sounds of Letty moving around the bed-

room. I deliberately waited until all sounds had ceased before I got out of the bath, as by now I had no desire for anything other than sleep, and the last thing I wanted was to get into another conversation.

I came back into the bedroom and opened the door to the sitting room to allow the flickering firelight to play upon the bedroom walls. I turned out the gas, leaving only a solitary candle burning by the bed. I was just about to climb between the sheets when I noticed something strange.

Nana was no longer there.

Chapter Three

FOR A MOMENT I was somewhat nonplussed. The bed had been turned down, and I had heard someone moving around while I was bathing. I had assumed that it must be Letty. Still, I thought that it was rather strange that Nana had been moved, particularly after some person had had the rather sweet thought of putting him in my room. It must have been put there by somebody who knew me well, who knew that ever since I was three I had always taken him to bed with me.

I searched the bedroom, not omitting the wardrobes. I looked carefully around the sitting room, but there was no sign of Nana. I felt vaguely uneasy, though why I could not see. After all, it was a small matter, and surely there was a perfectly rational explanation for the disappearance. "Emma," I told myself, "you are being a little fool." It was quite certain that Letty had taken Nana away when she had turned down the bed.

It was with this thought in mind that I finally clambered

between the sheets, sinking luxuriously into the huge, soft, feather mattress which billowed up on either side of me like a warm embracing wall. I gazed at the embroidery on the canopy over my head and gradually relaxed as drowsiness overcame me and I surrendered my body to sleep.

"Good morning, Miss Emma."

I opened my eyes, stretched, and listened for a moment to the swish of the curtains as they were drawn back. As the daylight flooded into the room, I blinked and eased myself into a sitting position, from which I observed a waiflike figure approaching the bed, carrying a pink knitted woolen bed jacket. She helped me into the jacket and stacked pillows behind me.

"Good morning," I replied sleepily. "You must be Letty." She was dressed in the traditional fashion of a lady's maid: black dress, white starched cap, and apron. Two huge brown eyes looked at me out of a thin pallid face, the sort of face that was so typical of working-class girls who spent their entire childhoods without ever having quite enough to eat. She was one of those, I supposed, who at the age of twelve were turned out into an unfriendly world where, if they were lucky, they secured for themselves a position "in service." Letty was one of the lucky ones. Looking at her, I supposed that she must be about fifteen. But she was already a lady's maid, a post which guaranteed her three good meals a day, a comfortable bed to sleep in, and about five pounds a year to spend or to send home to a mother who needed it more than she did.

"Yes, Miss Emma, I'm Letty," she replied, making a little bobbing curtsy. "Shall I bring your tea in now, or would you like it in the sitting room? I've lit the fire."

What luxury, I thought. I had forgotten the little things —like early morning tea served in one's room—which made Goathlands so comfortable and warm. What a lovely choice: tea in bed, or sitting in a dressing gown by a blazing fire? I thought for a moment and made my choice.

"I'll take tea in the sitting room," I said. "What is the weather like?"

"I think it's all right, miss," replied Letty.

"It looks a lovely day from here," I said, looking at the sunlight streaming through the windows.

"Yes, miss, it's a lovely day," she said. "I'll just go and get your tea, miss."

I was soon to discover that Letty would never answer a question until she was sure that she knew what answer one wanted to hear.

I got out of bed, put on my dressing gown, and went to the window. I gazed out at Goathlands moor, which rolled away into the distance, all warm and friendly in the autumn sunlight. Far away toward the horizon I could just make out the Roman road. This road was about two miles long. It started nowhere, went nowhere, and ended nowhere, but when it was first discovered it was hailed as one of the great archeological finds of the era. It was the most perfect example of Roman roadworks to be discovered outside of Italy. Its chipped and broken surface was carefully tended all the year 'round by Albert Higgins, whose sole occupation this was.

I heard the rattle of the tea tray in the sitting room and went through. Letty was placing my tray in front of the fire. It was then that I remembered Nana.

"Letty," I said. "Would you bring Nana back? And please don't take him away again."

"Nana, miss?" She looked at me blankly.

"Of course you wouldn't know his name," I replied. "I am referring to the teddy bear which was on my bed last night. I assume that you moved it when you turned the bed down."

"Teddy bear?" She looked startled. "I never saw no teddy bear, miss."

"Are you sure?" It was my turn to be puzzled.

"Honest, miss, there was no teddy bear here last night."

The girl was obviously frightened, and I tried to calm her. "Letty," I said firmly. "I am not suggesting anything. The teddy bear was on my bed when I went for my bath and it was gone when I returned. It was you who prepared my room last night?"

"Why, yes, miss, while you was in the bath, miss, but there was no teddy bear, I swear it, miss, I never seen no teddy bear."

"All right, Letty, you can go, and please don't worry about it." As she turned to go, a thought struck me. "Letty, was anyone else in my room last night?"

"Yes, miss, there must have been, miss."

"Who was it, Letty, did you see them?" I asked.

"No, miss, I didn't see nobody. Nobody had any cause to come here, but I didn't see no teddy bear."

"Very well, Letty, I believe you. Please don't worry about it."

Letty left me. Had she been lying? She had looked frightened, but then she was the sort who would always be frightened, especially if she thought that I was accusing her. Though I had certainly not intended any sort of accusation. But what had happened to Nana? If Letty had been telling the truth, then someone else had been in my room while I was in the bath. But who, and why? It all seemed so senseless.

With doubts and questions still gnawing at my mind, I finished my tea, dressed, and went downstairs to the dining room. No one seemed to be about, which did not surprise me as it was almost nine o'clock. Breakfast at Goathlands was always a very informal affair. A long hot plate was placed on the sideboard, and on top of this there would be up to half a dozen silver dishes containing breakfast comestibles such as sausages, kidneys, bacon, eggs, tomatoes, and kippers. There was always coffee. If you wanted tea you had to ring for it, and it was served fresh. The state of the servers confirmed my guess that I was the last one down. I helped myself to a generous portion of kidneys and tomatoes. I was really quite hungry and I finished them with relish. I noticed that the dining room clock said that it was now twenty minutes past nine o'clock.

I had over an hour before I was due to see Uncle Josh, so I decided to go and see if I could find Honey. I rang for Barton, who appeared almost immediately.

"Good morning, Miss Emma. Was there something you required?" he asked.

"Yes," I replied. "I wanted to ask you if you knew where Honey is."

"As far as I know, he'll be in one of the loose boxes behind the big barn, miss, unless he's been turned out into the small paddock. I do know that he isn't in the fields, because Sir Joshua arranged to have him brought in and shod as soon as he knew that you were coming."

"Thank you, Barton," I replied.

"Did you have sufficient breakfast, Miss Emma?"

"Thank you, it was lovely. I'm glad you remembered that I like kidneys."

"Oh, yes, miss, they'll always be there when you are at home. Will that be all, miss?"

"I think so," I replied. "Oh, if you can find a pair of wellingtons, would you leave them in the hall for me?"

I went up to my room and got a coat and muffler. Sure enough, the wellingtons were standing in the hall. I put them on and went out of the house.

I walked around the west wing toward the big barn. Looking up at the stout gray walls of Goathlands, I could see that they still bore the scars of that terrible fire. The scars were fading now, but here and there were still patches of wall which were scarred black. I thought of the inferno, savage enough to burn the stonework, in which my poor dear aunt had perished and in which my beloved Uncle Josh had been so cruelly disfigured.

But these were morbid thoughts, and I cheered myself up remembering that I was soon to see Honey again. When the big barn came in sight, I was surprised at the change in its appearance. It had never been a very pretty building, for it had been somewhat neglected. It had always looked its age, which must have been about fifty years. It was therefore with some astonishment that I saw that the building had been carefully restored and newly painted a bright green. In fact, it might have been a completely new barn, though it retained the old shape. Certainly the large sliding doors, whose runners projected beyond the eaves, were new.

The quickest way to the stables was through the big barn, and I saw that though the sliding doors were closed, one of them contained a small door through which a person might pass. I opened this and stepped inside.

The interior was quite dark, and I paused to allow my eyes to become accustomed to the gloom. I noticed a strange smell. It was rather like the smell of one of Uncle Joshua's horseless carriages mingled with something else, something oddly sweet and cloying. At the far end I could just discern a strange shape. It seemed to occupy quite a large amount of space, and it was certainly not a horseless carriage. I was just about to step toward it when a most terrifying sound greeted my ears.

A huge, almost black German shepherd confronted me. His ears were back, his hackles were up, and his upper lip was curled back, revealing a most dangerous-looking set of fangs. I froze in terror, staring at this great beast. Suddenly a voice called from the other end of the barn.

"Who the devil's that? Whoever you are, don't move and he won't attack you."

The dog growled, long and low and threatening. I heard footsteps approaching from the other end of the barn, and through the gloom a figure appeared. The figure gradually took on the shape of a tall, sandy-haired man dressed in white overalls, which were liberally smeared with some black substance.

"Sit, Basil," he commanded.

The dog sat down but did not for a moment take his eyes off me. The man glared at me, his eyes blazing. When he spoke, his voice was cultured, though the words he used were not the sort of language that a lady expects to hear.

"Who the blazes are you, and what do you think you are doing here?" he demanded.

"I am walking through the barn to the stables. As for what I am doing here, I happen to live here, and I can assure you that I am not accustomed to being addressed in such a cavalier fashion." I was really feeling quite indignant, but I never took my eyes off the dog.

"Don't worry about him. He won't touch you while I'm here. It's a jolly good job for you that you weren't here half an hour earlier, or you might have been badly mauled. All right, Basil, go to your house."

The dog obediently trotted off towards the other end of the barn.

"Now, young lady, I am sorry if you have had a fright, but no one, and by that I mean no one at all, is allowed in here. You would probably be quite surprised if you knew how many people would like to get in, but they are not going to. That is why we keep the dog. Now, please understand me, I don't care if you live here, I don't care if you are the Queen of England. I have a job to do and part of that job is to keep prying eyes away from our work; so nobody comes snooping around this barn, and that means you. Why don't you try to be a good little girl and run away and play somewhere else?"

I don't think that I have ever been so angry in my life. "Will you stand aside, sir?" I demanded.

"And just where do you think that you are going?"

"If it is any of your business, which I doubt, I am on my way to the stables," I answered with as much dignity as I could summon.

"Well, young lady, it so happens that it is my business, and if you want to go to the stables you can walk 'round the barn," he replied. "You are certainly not coming through here."

Really, his manner was most offensive. Even as a child I could not recall ever having been spoken to in such a manner.

"Please get out of my way," I said, taking a pace toward him.

"All right, you've asked for it," he said. "This way."

He stepped toward me and actually seized me by the elbow, turned me round, and marched me out of the door through which I had entered.

"Don't come back," he said.

There was no point in my trying to resist him, for he was obviously very strong. He put me outside and went back into the barn. I heard a bolt snap into place.

I swung round and glared at the now locked door. How I would have enjoyed teaching that young man a lesson in good manners. I was so furious that I was almost in tears. What had they to hide? And what was that mysterious shape at the far end of the barn? It began to dawn on me that perhaps I had made a mistake in coming to Goathlands after all.

"Is there something wrong, Miss Emma?"

I turned; it was Ormerod who was speaking to me. Here at least was a friend.

"Oh, Ormerod," I said, sniffling. I could feel the tears welling up in my eyes.

"Now, who's been making thee cry, Miss Emma?" It

was the same Ormerod that I used to run to when, as a child, I had been scolded and felt miserable.

"I'm not crying," I whimpered.

"No, of course thou are not crying," he replied.

"Ormerod, who is that awful man in there?"

"Oh, that would be Mr. Roger. I don't rightly know, Miss Emma. Very strange he is, he doesn't talk to anybody and of course none of us is allowed in there. Sir Joshua knows all about it, of course. Thou'll have to ask him if you want to know."

"I certainly shall ask him," I replied. "Your Mr. Roger is the rudest man I have ever met in my life."

So there was a secret at Goathlands. I did not like secrets, especially secrets that needed huge dogs to guard them. I would certainly ask Uncle Joshua and find out what it was all about, or I would not stay another day in this place.

"What are thou going to do now, then, Miss Emma?" asked Ormerod, breaking in on my thoughts.

"I have to see Uncle Josh at ten-thirty. I had hoped that I should be able to see Honey before then. I was on my way through the barn when that awful man and his dog threw me out."

"Well, miss, thou has still got plenty of time to see Honey; he's in the small paddock. I saw him there earlier on. I tell thee what, why don't I walk round with thee?"

"I suppose you couldn't take me through the barn?" I murmured. No one would dare molest me if I was with Ormerod.

"Nay, lass, 'tis more than my job's worth. Come with me and I'll take thee round. Have tha' brought his apple?"

I had forgotten the apple, but Omerod soon put that right. He produced a pair of shiny red apples from his capacious pocket and handed them to me.

"Windfalls," he explained.

We walked around the big barn. It did not put more than fifty paces onto the journey, but I resented every step. All the way I felt angry and frustrated that we were not going through the barn.

"There he is, miss." Ormerod pointed. "I'll be off now, I'd better be about my work."

Sure enough, there was Honey, head down, munching away at the grass. He was on the far side of the paddock, looking as beautiful as ever. I leaned against the gate, looking at him for a moment. His winter coat had not yet started to grow, and he still looked sleek and shiny and well cared for. A little fat, perhaps, but a few days' work would soon fine him down.

"Honey," I called.

He lifted his head and pricked his ears.

"Honeybunch."

This time he looked toward me. I could feel the butterflies in my tummy. I did so want him to remember me, but it had been eight years, and eight years is a long time by any standards.

"Honey, Honey, come on, boy, don't you remember me?" I was going to hold up the apples, but I managed to restrain myself. He would most certainly have come for an apple, but I wanted him to come for me.

He stared at me for what seemed an age, and then suddenly, something must have clicked in his mind. He tossed his head a couple of times and then trotted toward me. I thought that he was coming, but about ten paces from me he stopped and his ears went back as he scrutinized me once more. My heart sank; perhaps he was not going to recognize me after all.

"Please try and remember me, Honey," I pleaded. "Honeybunch, come on, boy."

It was going to be all right. He tossed his head and gave a little whinny of pleasure and almost pushed me off my feet as he nosed his soft muzzle into my shoulder. I climbed the gate, sat on the top bar, produced the apples, and fed them to him. In the paddock, we walked and talked, his head over my shoulder, as we had done so often before, so many years ago. I think for the first time since I had arrived I felt the thrill of real pleasure.

Soon, too soon it seemed, our pleasant little sojourn was over. It was time to go back to the house and keep my appointment with Uncle Josh. I said goodbye to Honey and turned to go. On the way back I felt the indignation rising within me as I skirted the big barn. I glared at it and heaped mental maledictions on the offensive Mr. Roger who was within. I got back to the house and took my wellingtons off in the hall. It was a rule we had followed as children—always to return a borrowed article to its place of origin. I ran upstairs, took off my coat and muffler, and, after a quick glance in the mirror to make sure that I was presentable, made my way toward the west wing.

A tiny feeling of apprehension came over me when I found myself once more outside Uncle Josh's room, but I disregarded it. Just as the clock chimed the half hour, I tapped on the door, feeling quite proud of my punctuality.

"Enter."

Uncle Josh was sitting in one of the armchairs beside the fire. I was quite relieved to see that he was alone, wearing a brown skullcap and a patch over his right eye. I think he must have noticed my reaction to this, for he said, "I suppose that I look a little like a pirate, but I'm sure that you'll find it much easier to work with."

"I don't mind, Uncle, honestly I don't." On impulse, I leaned over and kissed him on the cheek.

He raised his hand to the spot my lips had touched. "It's a long time since anyone did that to me. Thank you, my dear."

"But I love you, Uncle, I always have. You have had an awful time, but you are still Uncle Josh."

"I hope so, Emma, anyway I shall try to be. My dear, I

want you to be happy at Goathlands, and you are to feel quite free to come and see me at any time. I have given instructions to Dr. Harrison to this effect. She's a bit of a watchdog, you know, but she does look after me. Anyway, she is now aware of your position in the household. Well, Emma," he said, his tone changing and becoming more businesslike, "I suppose that you are wondering what all of this is about, eh?"

"As a matter of fact, I am," I replied, my mind going back to the incident in the big barn.

"Then my first task is to explain, and insofar as I am able, to put you in the picture. First, as I have already explained, I want you to regard yourself as mistress here. This is, after all, no more than your rightful position, at least as long as Henry remains unmarried. Now, far be it from me to even attempt to explain your duties in that department. As a mere man, I have little or no knowledge of how to run a house."

I smiled, for did he but know it, his knowledge must have been at least as great as mine; I had never run any establishment larger than my two-roomed flat in London.

"Dr. Harrison has been very helpful in that department," he continued, "and between her, Barton, and Cook, I am quite sure that you will be able to deal with any problems which may arise." He paused for a moment and then went on. "The other part of your duties does, however, concern me directly, and the first thing I must make clear is that they are most secret and are not to be discussed with anyone other than myself or Mr. Attwood."

"Mr. Attwood?" I asked.

"Yes, I think that you had better meet him right away. Perhaps you would be kind enough to ring."

I pulled the tapestry bell rope and Dr. Harrison came in.

"Doctor," said my uncle, "would you send a message

to Mr. Attwood and ask him to step over here for a moment."

Dr. Harrison, thin-lipped and unsmiling, nodded and left.

"Please do not think that I treat Dr. Harrison as a servant," explained Uncle Joshua. "It is her own wish that she should wait upon me. She feels that rather than have someone call her when I need her urgently in her medical capacity, she would prefer to answer all my calls herself."

I could not help wondering whether those really were the lady's motives, or whether there was something more sinister. Perhaps it was her intention to make Uncle Josh so dependent on her that she did in fact control him.

"Well, now, where were we?"

"You were about to explain my duties apart from the running of the house," I replied.

"Oh, yes, and while it is on my mind, there will be a dinner party on Tuesday next. There will be four guests. That will make your table eight."

"Oh dear, not eight," I said. Even I knew that it was impossible to seat eight for dinner in the correct order. You just had to have two gentlemen and two ladies sitting together.

"Don't you worry about the eight," said Uncle Josh. "Your four guests are all men. Just as soon as Mr. Attwood gets here we'll explain to you about Kittiwake."

There was a tap at the door.

"Enter," said Uncle Josh.

The door opened and a man walked into the room. As our eyes met he glared at me.

"Great Scott! You again!" he roared.

Chapter Four

IT WAS ROGER. The revolting Roger, though I must say that he did not look revolting; far from it. He must have been all of six feet tall. He had sandy hair that looked as if it had a mind of its own, for as he stopped and stared at me, a lock fell across his brow and he brushed it back with his hand, only to have it return immediately to its former position. His eyes were light blue, almost grey, and they seemed to look through you with an intensity which was really quite unnerving. I particularly noticed his hands. They were big and strong, a peasant's hands like Ormerod's. But when he spoke it was with the cultured tones of a gentleman. Altogether, though I was loath to admit it, he was a most attractive looking man. What a pity, I thought, that apart from his greasy overalls, his manners did not match his appearance.

"What's this?" said Uncle Josh. "Have you two already met?"

"We have," replied Roger grimly.

"I have never been introduced to this," I paused deliberately before saying the word, "gentleman."

"Like that, is it," said Uncle Josh knowingly. "Well, I'd better introduce you now. Emma, this is my associate, Mr. Roger Attwood. Roger, this is my niece, Miss Emma Waldron."

"How do you do," said Mr. Attwood with a formality that was quite insulting.

"I am very well, thank you," I replied, taking his tone. "I am, however, none the better for my experience this

38

morning, for which I trust that you will now have the grace to apologize."

"No, Miss Waldron, I shall not apologize." The beast had the impertinence to smile at me. "No one is allowed in the big barn, and in removing you I was simply doing my job, and I am sorry to have to say that. Even had I known at the time who you are, I should still have ejected you."

The man really was insufferable.

"Now then, what is all this?" Uncle Josh demanded.

"I am sorry, Sir Joshua," explained Mr. Attwood. "Miss Waldron came into the big barn this morning, I suppose it was about an hour ago, and to put it in a nutshell, I threw her out."

"Physically," I snapped.

"I doubt if there was any other way in which I could have persuaded you to leave."

"You are no gentleman," I said. "You manhandled me."

"True," he replied. "But was there any other way to get rid of you?"

I remained silent.

"Now listen, you two," said Uncle Josh. "There's no point in starting off with a flaming row. You're going to be working together a lot, whether you like it or not. You might just as well be pleasant to one another, and for a start, I suggest that, however uncalled for, you, Roger, apologize, and you, Emma, accept that apology with good grace." We both hesitated. "Come now, I insist."

"I'm sorry," said Roger, without conviction.

"I accept your apology, Mr. Attwood," I replied formally.

"Well, if that's the best you can do, I don't think much of it," said Uncle Josh. "But I suppose that it will have to do for now. Now, sit down, the pair of you, and listen to me."

"I think I'd better take these off first, sir, hadn't I?" said

Roger, indicating his grease-smeared white overalls.

"Pull up a chair and sit down as you are," said Uncle Josh. "A touch of grease around the place will make me feel more at home. Now then, Roger, how are things going in your department?"

"Not too badly, sir," he replied. "I'm still having a bit of trouble with the control wires for the ailerons."

"I thought you might," said Uncle Josh. "I might have to change their geometry. Bring the drawings over this afternoon and I'll see what I can work out."

"What about?" asked Roger, giving a significant glance in my direction.

"And what, pray, do you mean by that remark, sir?" I bridled.

"All right, all right," said Uncle Josh. "You need have no worries about Emma. From now on she is one of us and privy to all our secrets. This is the reason I sent for you. I thought that you two ought to meet and I felt that it would be a good thing if you, Roger, were present during this conversation. Now, Emma, I suppose that you would like to hear about Kittiwake?"

"Kittiwake?" I asked, somewhat puzzled. I knew, of course, what a kittiwake was. Kittiwakes are among the most common of the sea gulls which are found on our part of the North Sea coast. "Is this to do with birds?"

"Yes, my dear, very special birds," replied Uncle Josh. "Birds that men can ride upon. We are building a flying machine."

I could not but be thrilled at the idea. There was a great deal of talk in those days about flying machines. Only last summer, Monsieur Blériot had surprised the whole world when he flew his flying machine across the English Channel in, I believe, little more than half an hour. On the other hand, I was not really surprised to discover that Uncle Josh was interested in this sort of adventure. After all, he

had always been much taken by all things mechanical, and
it was not to be wondered at that he had turned his atten-
tions to this latest sport.

"A flying machine," I said. "This is truly exciting."

"We started some time ago," Uncle Josh continued. "I
have incorporated in the design of Kittiwake some rather
revolutionary new ideas, and I am sure that these will provide a basis for a great step forward in the evolution of
powered flight. Roger here has helped a great deal, quite
apart from actually building her, and, of course, he will be
the one to fly her. I hope that she will be ready for her
maiden flight next Wednesday."

"Uncle Josh," I said as he paused. "All of this is wonderful news, but I cannot for the life of me see what need
you can have for a woman. All this strikes me as very
much a male reserve."

"Ah, but we do need you, Emma,'" replied Uncle Josh.
"You will no doubt recall that I told you that there would
be four guests at dinner on Tuesday. Well, these gentlemen are all important, high ranking officers from the
army. You see, my dear, we are no longer convinced that
the flying machine is merely a sport. If we are right, it has
great military potential. Balloons are already in constant
use, and just think how much more efficient a free ranging
machine would be as it soared high above the field of bat-
tle where nothing could be hidden from the eyes of the
aeronaut. I'm sorry, I'm digressing, and when I do that I
tend to wax lyrical.

"On Tuesday, when these gentlemen arrive, I want each
of them to have a copy of the specifications of Kittiwake,
and, in addition, a copy of a rather lengthy paper which I
have prepared concerning the potential of the machine.
These documents will be studied by them on the Tuesday
night, and on Wednesday, weather permitting, they will be
able to observe the maiden flight.

"What I want you to do, Emma, is to typewrite all of these documents so that they can be presented in an orderly and legible manner. There are about forty-five pages altogether and, as I do not want them to receive copies, they will have to be typewritten out four times with absolute accuracy. I have recently taken delivery of a typewriting machine from the United States of America. I am assured that the model which I have secured is the finest available. This will be placed in your sitting room this morning. Now, do you think that you will be able to complete this on time? I would like to have the completed work not later than noon on Tuesday."

It was a lot, but I knew that I could manage. "I'm sure I can, uncle," I replied. "I'll make a start immediately after lunch."

"Good girl," he said. "Now, Roger, if you would kindly get the papers from my bureau, we can let Emma have them."

"As you say, sir," replied Roger. "By the way, Miss Waldron, it is important that these papers be kept under lock and key. By this time next week they could be subject to the Official Secrets Act."

"I am sure that no one will come prying into my rooms," I retorted. "But I will do as you request."

I spoke with more conviction than I felt. Official Secrets had an ominous ring to it, and I could not help thinking of the mysterious disappearance of Nana. I was on the point of telling them about this, but, realizing that it might sound silly and trivial, I held my counsel.

"Don't be too sure about anything," said Roger. "Your uncle is not unknown as an inventor, and there could be more than a few unscrupulous persons who would be more than happy to steal his secrets."

"Apart from anything else, Emma," said Uncle Josh, "this could be a matter of importance to the security of

England. Roger is quite right, we must take no unnecessary risks."

Roger handed me a large bundle of papers tied up with white tape.

"Here you are, Miss Waldron. You will find that all the technical terms have been written out in block letters, so you should have no queries. But, if you do and don't want to disturb Sir Joshua, you will find me in the barn. If you should have cause to come there, please knock. I'd hate to have Basil think you were his supper." He grinned.

I turned to Uncle Joshua. "Is there anything else?" I asked, ignoring Roger's remarks.

"No, I think that is all," replied my uncle. "I suppose you'll want to be getting along now?"

As I rose to go I heard him ask Roger to stay with him a while and discuss the problem of the ailerons. I took my leave of them and left the room.

"Miss Waldron?"

The corridor outside Uncle Joshua's room was very dimly lit, and for a moment I could not see where the whispered remark had come from. Then I made out a shadowy figure standing just to the left of Uncle Joshua's door. It was Dr. Harrison.

"Miss Waldron, I should like to have a word with you, if that would be convenient."

I was really quite startled. I got the feeling that she had been there for some time. Doing what? I asked myself. All this talk about official secrets, and here was someone who had been standing right outside the door. For how long? She might well have been eavesdropping on our conversation.

"Is it important?" I asked.

"In my opinion it is," replied Dr. Harrison. "If you would step into my room for a moment, there is something I want to tell you. My room is just here across the corridor from Sir Joshua."

I could not very well refuse her request. She opened a door and ushered me into a large, well-lighted room, one part of which had been equipped with the usual paraphernalia and furnishings which one would expect to find in a doctor's surgery. I also noticed a fairly large glass-fronted cabinet containing various bottles labelled with Latin names, which I assumed to be her stock of medicines and drugs.

"Do sit down, Miss Waldron." It was a command rather than a request. "If there is anything you have to be getting on with, please do not worry. I shall not detain you for long."

"What is it you want, doctor?" I inquired, sitting down and clutching my bundle of papers.

"I considered it necessary to have a word with you about Sir Joshua. You are fond of your uncle. This is true, is it not?"

"I love him very dearly, I always have done, ever since I was a little girl. He has always been a great favorite of mine," I replied.

"In that case, I am quite sure that you will take heed of what I have to say to you. I know a great deal about your uncle, probably more than anyone since his wife died. There is, however, one aspect of his life which is a closed book to me. That part of his life which concerns his work, he keeps completely secret from me. Now I am going to be perfectly frank with you. I have, in spite of his prohibition, attempted to find out about his work; not because I am interested in it per se, but because I know that it excites him and I also know that excitement is not good for him.

"The tragedy of two years ago left him a very sick man. Quite apart from the disfigurement that he suffered, he has been left with a weak heart. Now, and I want you to understand this, it is my job to look after him. He pays me well, treats me as one of the family, and though he is my patient, I feel both friendship and admiration for him. I must insure that he is subject to no undue stress or excitement, and in this it has become quite obvious that I shall need your help.

"I have no intention of asking you to betray any confidences, though as a doctor, I am not unaccustomed to receiving confidences and respecting them. I am, however, going to ask you to try not to worry him, and if ever you are in doubt, be it ever so small, I want you to consult me. It would be better if you could manage to see me before visiting him. He does have his off periods when I would prefer him to be left quite alone."

As she spoke, she fingered the cameo on her dress. I must have been staring at it, for she continued, "I see that you recognize this brooch."

"Yes, I do," I replied. "It used to belong to my aunt."

"That is quite true. Your uncle gave it to me and asked me to wear it whenever I was attending him. I believe that his wife wore it constantly, and he had a desire to see it frequently. I did not approve of the idea, but he is an emotional man, so under the circumstances, and because he insisted, I agreed to do as he asked."

A bell tinkled somewhere in the room.

"That is your uncle now, I must go to him. Please think about what I have said. I would appreciate an answer soon."

She left the room behind me. I was quite relieved that I was not required to answer her right away. I secretly blessed Uncle Josh for ringing when he did.

I walked slowly back to my rooms, thinking about what had happened; it had certainly been an eventful morning. First there had been the row with Roger in the barn. I was quite determined that, come what may, I was not going to like that young man. In spite of his good looks he was brusque to the point of rudeness. Then there was Honey, yes, that had been nice. He was still my friend; he still knew me. It was a pity that I would not be able to ride him over the weekend, but I was committed to doing all of this typewriting for Uncle Joshua and that would take nearly all my time. And now this interview with Dr. Harrison. She was a strange woman—she seemed cold and dispassionate, and yet her words had indicated a genuine concern for Uncle Joshua. On the other hand, it was obvious that Uncle Josh had kept her in the dark about Kittiwake. Was she appearing solicitous in the hope that I would betray my trust? Could she be one of the unscrupulous persons to whom Roger had referred when he was talking about the need for security? She had certainly succeeded in placing me in a quandary, for if I made her my confidante, I should be betraying my trust, and if I did not, I might be risking the well-being, even the life, of Uncle Josh.

"Wake up or you'll miss lunch."

In my preoccupation I had almost walked into Henry.

"What have you got there, coz?" he asked, indicating the papers I was clutching. "The crown jewels?"

"Oh!" I said, startled. "These? Just some work for Uncle Josh."

"To do with the secret of the big barn, I'll warrant," he said, smiling.

"I . . . I'm not sure what you are talking about," I replied, somewhat flustered. I had no idea how much, if anything, Henry was supposed to know. "I'll just go and put these in my room and then I'll join you for lunch."

"Allow me to carry them for you," he offered, reaching out his hand.

"No, thank you," I answered, clutching my precious papers still tighter, and with that I fled to my room.

In my sitting room I found a magnificent new typewriting machine which had been placed on top of a stout oaken desk cupboard. I put the papers inside the cupboard and locked it. The key also fitted the center drawer, which contained paper, erasers, and a brush for cleaning the type. I locked the drawer and looked around for a place to keep the key. There was an empty powder bowl on the dressing table in my bedroom, so I placed the key in that until such time as I could find a more suitable place. I had just finished doing this when I heard the distant sound of the gong. It was time for luncheon.

I walked down to the dining room, and for the first time, I took my place at the head of the table as mistress of Goathlands.

Luncheon was a quiet meal. Henry sat at the far end of the table with Dr. Harrison on his right. Roger, who it appeared ate en famille, was late; he arrived halfway through the soup and placed himself on my right. The meal was served quietly and efficiently by Barton, who whispered to me that he would like me to meet the rest of the servants that afternoon and that Mrs. Jollyman, our cook, would like to see me some time that day to discuss Tuesday's menu.

Dr. Harrison ate her meal in stony silence, excusing herself before the dessert was served. Roger Attwood made one or two attempts to open a conversation with me, but I was still angry at the way he had treated me earlier and I responded very coolly. All of this seemed to amuse Henry, who kept up a constant chatter about trivialities such as the weather and Yorkshire's performance in the county cricket championships that summer.

Luncheon over, I rose to leave them. They stood as I made my way to the door. I was just about to go out when Henry spoke.

"You wouldn't care to go for a stroll this afternoon?" he asked.

"I am sorry," I replied. "But I have far too much work to do."

"Pity," he answered, and then added with a chuckle, "I'm going to look at some birds . . . sea gulls, you know."

Chapter Five

HENRY'S REMARK STOPPED me, but only for a moment. I think that he was trying to tell me that the great secret was not really so much of a secret after all. This was not too surprising, since he lived here. He must have seen goings on from which, being a person of reasonable intelligence, he had drawn his own conclusions. Henry always made this sort of remark with a kind of light sarcastic humor which was typical of him. It was not unpleasant and certainly not unreasonable. He was, and there was no doubt about this, being kept in the dark about his own father's work. Could it be that Uncle Joshua did not altogether trust his son? And if he did not trust him, was there any reason for it? If there was no reason, then why this strange desire for secrecy?

Anyhow, I told myself, it was none of my business. I had a job to get on with and should not be spending my time in idle speculation.

I went straight up to my sitting room and started work. Though the work itself was not very interesting, the typewriting machine was a joy to use, quite the finest I had ever had. The papers I had to copy contained a great many technical terms which I did not understand, words which I had to spell out because I had never heard them before. Apart from these words, my fingers flew over the keyboard, and I soon realized that it would be quite within my capabilities to have the whole thing finished some time on Monday afternoon. This would be most convenient, as it would leave me all of Tuesday free to prepare for the dinner party that evening. I could have finished earlier than Monday afternoon, but the morrow being Sunday, I would of course be going to church, and that would occupy most of the morning.

At about four o'clock, by which time I was well into my task, Letty brought afternoon tea up to my sitting room. How lovely it looked: tea, hot muffins oozing freshly churned farm butter, cucumber sandwiches, and to complete the nostalgia, three little cakes covered with pink icing and a cherry sitting on top of each one.

"Where will you be taking your tea, miss?" asked Letty.

"Put it on the table by the fire," I replied.

"Was there anything else, miss?"

"No, that will be all, thank you, Letty." Then I remembered Nana. "By the way, Letty, I suppose you didn't by any chance find my teddy bear?" I inquired.

"No, miss, I told you, miss, I never seen your teddy bear, miss." The words tumbled out as if she was defending herself against a charge of theft.

"All right, Letty," I said soothingly. "Don't let it worry you. I suppose that it will turn up somewhere."

"You don't think that I . . . ?" She looked so frightened that I felt really sorry for her.

"Of course not, Letty, what reason could you possibly have? Now, please don't worry about it." I smiled at her. "You can run along now . . . and Letty . . ."

She turned at the door. "Yes, miss?"

"Thank you for bringing my tea."

She smiled her thin little smile and left me. She was obviously very much relieved.

I spent a leisurely half hour over my tea and then went down below stairs to meet the rest of the staff and to renew my acquaintanceship with fat, jovial Mrs. Jollyman,

our cook, with whom I discussed the menu for Tuesday.
"Discussed" is probably the wrong word, for Mrs. Jollyman told me what we were going to have, pausing every
now and then to allow me to say, "Yes."

By five o'clock I was back at work, and apart from
three-quarters of an hour or so for dinner, I worked right
through until about eleven o'clock. By that time I had got
through about a third of the typewriting, and with the feeling of a good day's work behind me, I retired to bed with
a clear conscience.

Sunday dawned bright and sunny, and after a breakfast
consisting of those wonderful Yorkshire kippers, which
are unsurpassed anywhere in the world, I dressed for
church. I wore a dusty blue worsted skirt with a matching
tailored jacket over a lace blouse. I also wore a hat of dark
blue velour, over which passed a broad, wine-colored velvet ribbon tied in a bow under my chin.

Promptly at ten-thirty the landau was drawn up in front
of the house. I was glad it was not one of Uncle Joshua's
horseless carriages; it was probably much safer, too, as
there would be a lot of horses at the church. Ormerod was
waiting by the landau dressed in his Sunday best, which
included doeskin breeches, a black jacket, and a top hat.
He had to wear a top hat on formal occasions, of course,
but it always looked completely out of place over that
weatherbeaten countryman's face. We assembled in the
hall, both Henry and Roger looking very handsome in
their gray frock coats and top hats. Dr. Harrison was
wearing a black tweed coat over her black gown. I never
saw her in anything other than black, and I wondered if
she possessed any colored garments at all.

Roger confined his greeting to a grunted, "Good morning," while Henry saluted me handsomely and told me
how attractive I looked. I could not help warming to
Henry's flattery, and, on the other hand, feeling somewhat
snubbed by Roger's attitude. I wondered, did Roger really

dislike me or resent my presence here? I was rapidly coming to the conclusion that something of that sort must be the case.

We boarded the landau, and Ormerod took his place and cracked his whip. The matched pair of glossy black hackneys set off at a brisk high-stepping trot, and we were on our way.

Though it is little more than two miles, it is a beautiful run from the house to Goathland Village. After leaving the house, you go down a steep hill called "Two Howes Rigg." At the bottom, you join the road proper at Scar Wood. From there the road follows Wheeldale Beck—beck is the Yorkshire name for a large stream—as far as Mallyan Spout. Then the road leaves the beck and cuts across country for the last half mile to the village.

I was sitting on Henry's left, which meant that I had Roger facing me. During the entire journey, which took fifteen to twenty minutes, neither Roger nor Dr. Harrison said a word, while Henry chattered away a lot of inconsequential pleasantries. During the journey he slipped into my hand a beautiful *Book of Common Prayer*. I recognized it. It had belonged to my aunt. It was bound in mother-of-pearl, and I know that it had been one of her most treasured possessions.

"I thought you might like to have this," said Henry.

I smiled my thanks. How kind of him to think of that. I wondered why it was that my uncle had never really got on with his son. Granted, there was little depth to his conversation, but this was a very thoughtful gesture and he had at least shown some desire to make me feel at home.

At last the old Norman church came into view. As it was not more than a few minutes before eleven o'clock, we went straight in. We took our places in the family pew, which was at the left front of the nave, just below the pulpit. I remembered how, as a child, I had always wished that our place had been further back. Sitting there under the ever-watchful eye of our vicar, the Reverend Cox, it was impossible to suck an illegal candy or to let my attention wander. If I did, the vicar would most surely bring my indiscretions to the notice of my parents or, more frightening still, my nanny.

The morning service over, we filed out of church, where the vicar was waiting to greet us all individually. To me he gave a particularly warm welcome and promised that he would call and pay his respects at the earliest possible moment.

Ormerod, who had been sitting toward the rear of the church with the rest of our staff, was already waiting at the landau. He put the step down for me to enter when I suddenly realized that Henry was not with us.

"Have you seen Henry?" I asked.

"No, miss," replied Ormerod. "He should be with you."

"Unless I am mistaken, that is your cousin over there," said Dr. Harrison, speaking for, I think, the first time since we had left Goathlands.

I looked in the direction which she had indicated, and sure enough, there he was, deep in conversation with a man that I had never seen before. I had no idea who this stranger was, but he did not strike me as looking like the sort of person with whom I would expect my cousin to associate. His dress, though obviously expensive, was in the most appalling taste; dark grey breeches, a loud check jacket, and a brown bowler hat. Henry seemed to be in a heated argument with him, and though I was too far away to hear the conversation, it was obvious that an angry exchange was taking place. It was when the man clenched his fist and shook it under Henry's chin that Roger took a hand.

"Wait here, ladies," he said. "I think I'd better go and sort this out."

It was a good thing that he did, as by that time several members of the congregation were watching with that morbid interest which a row always seems to stimulate.

Roger walked purposefully over and stood between them. I saw him say something to Henry, and then he turned to the other man and spoke to him. The man responded by waving his arms about and wagging an accusing finger at Henry. Roger then turned again to Henry, who nodded. Then, as Roger continued talking, Henry shook his head. Roger took his wallet out of his purse and took from it some pieces of paper; they were white and could have been five pound notes, though I was not close enough to be sure. Roger thrust the papers into the man's top breast pocket. The man turned on his heel, taking the paper out of his pocket as he did so, and walked away. For a moment Henry seemed to hesitate as Roger appeared to try and persuade him to rejoin us. Finally, both men returned to the landau. Henry was flushed with embarrassment and breathing heavily as he took his place beside me, while Roger, cool and unruffled, sat down and ordered Ormerod to drive us home.

The journey home was a silent one. Try as I might I could read nothing into the expressions of my companions. Roger was cool and collected, Henry was obviously in a fearsome temper, and Dr. Harrison was as calm and impassive as ever.

When we arrived at the house, Henry leapt from the landau and dashed up the steps and indoors without a word. Roger waited for the doctor and myself to alight and then escorted us inside.

"How's the work going?" he asked.

I was amazed. It was the first civilized remark he had made to me. But I had no intention of letting him think that I was at all interested in his concern.

"It will be completed on time," I replied coldly.

He grinned and left us. Dr. Harrison turned to me and said, "Please do not make any mention of this morning's incident to your uncle."

Of course I had no intention of doing anything of the sort, but I was curious. So, after assuring her that I would say nothing to Uncle Joshua, I asked her if she knew who the strange man was, or if she knew the reason for his accosting Henry.

"I am afraid that I know nothing about it," she replied.

Frankly, I did not believe her. Had she been a normal person I would have said that this was not the first time that she had witnessed such a scene. Roger also was obviously aware of the facts and not surprised by them. All sorts of explanations came to mind: blackmail, gambling, money-lenders? I could make no sense of it. In any case, I had work to do, so I went upstairs and back to my type-writing.

I set to work with furious energy. I think I was trying to drive from my mind all thought of the unpleasantness outside the church. But my thoughts continued to nag away at me. Typewriting from copy is not a great mental exercise, and after one has gotten into the swing of it it becomes almost automatic. As the machine rattled away, I found my thoughts wandering over the situation at Goathlands.

For myself, I felt completely isolated; what I really needed was a friend. I wanted someone in whom I could confide, someone whom I could trust to listen, with sympathy and understanding, to the strange story of Nana's disappearance. My mind traveled first, of course, to Uncle Josh. It would not be the first time that I had taken my troubles to him. He, I knew, was a friend. But on the other hand, Dr. Harrison had warned me against bothering him. For his own sake, I could not ignore that. It appeared that his need of solicitude and consideration was much greater than mine.

Then there was the lady doctor herself. I had the impression that she would repel any advance, on any plane, other than those of a purely professional nature. I felt that she did not like me. She was a forbidding, enigmatic sort of person, yet she had indicated that she was fond of Uncle Josh, and her actions gave me no reason to believe otherwise. Whether she liked me or not was a matter of little moment. All of this, assuming it to be true, meant that I had no alternative but to respect her advice. That she was a good doctor was beyond doubt. Uncle Josh would never have engaged her had this not been the case. Though my grandfather's considerable fortune was held in trust for Henry and myself, Uncle Josh had the income from it and could certainly afford the best.

Henry, of course, was family. He was kind and considerate, and the little gesture of the prayer book that morning was the sort of thing which made me feel warm and affectionate towards him. Warm and affectionate yes, but trusting was something else. I could not understand why, but there was something inside of me which said no, when reason dictated that I should confide in him. Was it his occasionally sardonic humor? Was it because Uncle Josh did not seem to trust him? Or was it because of the incident I had witnessed outside the church? I did not know the answers, and, not knowing, I could not take a chance and open my heart to him.

Ormerod was a friend, but not the sort of friend who would understand a woman's secret fears. I knew that I could trust Ormerod, but he would have regarded a story about a disappearing teddy bear as a joke. Perhaps he would have been right in that. If, on the other hand, I had wanted a yeoman to slay a dragon or to save me from physical harm, I knew that Ormerod would lay down his life for me, but subtleties would always escape him. He was of the earth, earthy.

Roger, of course, was impossible.

But these were foolish thoughts. They all stemmed from the vanishing Nana, an incident which certainly had a simple, logical explanation. I paused in my work and walked over to the window.

The moors looked beautiful bathed in the autumn sunlight. "You little fool," I said aloud. "You are letting yourself get into a state of nerves over nothing at all. Look out there, look at God's beautiful world, look around you at the warmth and security of your home. There's nothing to worry about."

I went back to my typewriting with a contented heart and rattled away happily at my work.

It was about three o'clock on Monday afternoon when I typed the last page of the last copy of my task. I assembled my work neatly and placed the copies in manilla folders. The copies I locked in the cupboard of my desk, the original manuscript I placed in the drawer, locking that also. I put the key back into the powder bowl and decided that, after spending the best part of three days hunched over my machine, a good brisk walk was what I needed. The weather was still fine, but by late afternoon there could be a nip in the air, so I slipped into a tweed jacket and a pair of stout walking shoes and set off, deciding to deliver the work to Uncle Joshua upon my return.

I walked out of the house and went west across Howl Moor and down the hill towards Wheeldale Beck. I crossed the beck on the stepping stones which had been there for as long as anyone could remember. The stones were worn smooth by the water and by the feet of generations of children. The children used to skip to and fro across the stones, calling, "Tinker, tailor, soldier, sailor, rich man, poor man, beggar man, thief." If you stepped on each stone, you always ended up with a "beggar man," but we all used to cheat a little and try to jump over a couple of stones without touching them, thus ending up with a "rich man" as we stepped onto the far bank. This, of course, was not without risk, and many a child would end up with a ducking. Today all was well, and I was saying "rich man" as I stepped onto the far bank.

I decided to walk on to the Roman Road, which ended about a quarter of a mile from where I had crossed.

"Bless my soul, if it isn't Miss Emma. We haven't seen you in these parts for many a year."

It was Mr. Higgins. As always, he was at work, weeding and clearing the flints and the slabs of stone along which, two thousand years ago, Caesar's legions had marched. It was said that on a still night, when the mist came down over the moors, you could still sometimes hear the tramp of their feet and the clatter of their weapons as they marched north toward the Tyne and Hadrian's Wall.

I stopped and chatted for a while with Mr. Higgins. But I soon decided that it must be time to be getting back, so I turned and retraced my steps toward Goathlands.

I had been rather longer than I had intended, and it was about five o'clock when I got back to the house. I went straight to my rooms and took off my outer garments. It was with a feeling of achievement that I went to get the typewritten copies from my desk. I opened the powder bowl and was much surprised to find that it was full of powder. I dug around with my fingers in the powder but the key was not there. That foolish girl Letty must have filled the bowl and removed the key, I thought. I went into the sitting room and was just about to ring for her when I noticed, to my astonishment, that the key was right there in the lock of the cupboard door.

It was with a feeling approaching panic that I went toward the desk. I reached out to the cupboard door. It was unlocked. I was becoming really afraid by this time. Someone had opened the cupboard. I swung the door open and stared in horror at the sight that confronted me.

Where I had left my beautifully typewritten manuscripts, there was now nothing but a pile of charred burnt paper.

I fell to my knees and wept bitterly.

Chapter Six

How LONG I lay there sobbing, I shall never know. The
next thing that I became aware of was that the light was
fading. I rose unsteadily to my feet and looked again at
the poor charred remains of my work. For a moment I
hoped that it might merely be some horrid practical joke,
but no; as I sifted through the ashes, I found pathetic little
scraps of unburnt paper which told me all too clearly that
it was indeed my precious work.

Dear God, I thought, the original! The original repre-
sented months, even years, perhaps, of Uncle Joshua's
painstaking research; had it been destroyed too? Had the
villain who had burnt my papers—for there could be no
doubt that this was a deliberate act—had that evil person
destroyed the original as well?

I tugged at the drawer where I had left it, but it was still
locked. I began to hope. I took the key out of the cupboard and, hardly daring to look, opened the drawer. It
was all right. The manuscript was still there, lying neatly
and safely where I had left it. Whoever it was that had
done this terrible deed had intended to give vent to his
hatred on me and on me alone.

But who? Who could it be? And why? What possible
reason could anyone have? Could it possibly be someone
like Letty? Could it be someone who resented people like
myself because we had the good fortune to be born into
good circumstances? Someone hated me, there could be
no doubt about that, but for what reason I could not imagine. It was now quite apparent that the disappearance of

Nana had been no accident, even though as a work of infamy, it could not compare with what had just happened.

But there were pressing and immediate problems. What could I do now? Uncle Joshua's guests would be arriving in the early evening of the next day. As Uncle Josh had told me, one of the prime purposes of their visit was to study the documents which I had been given the task of preparing for them. There was only one thing I could do. I would have to get down to it immediately and re-typewrite the whole lot.

In moments of great stress I had always found that action was the finest medicine, so it was with this thought in mind that I went into my bathroom and did a quick repair on my tear-streaked face. When I returned I found Letty in my sitting room.

"Letty," I asked as calmly as I could. "Have you been into this room since luncheon?"

"No, miss," she replied. "I'm sorry, miss, had you been wanting me, miss?"

I choked back the angry remarks that came tumbling to my lips. "No, Letty. Letty, I do not want to be disturbed this evening. You can tell Barton that I shall not be down to dinner. He can bring me a tray later."

"Yes, miss. What about your bed? Shall I do it now?" she replied.

"Never mind about my bed," I snapped, thinking that I should be lucky if I were to see my bed that night. "You can go now, and you can take the evening off."

"Oh, thank you, miss." She seemed pleased. "Have I done something right?"

"Letty, I just don't want to be disturbed. Please go now."

She left. The foolish girl was actually behaving as if I was rewarding her. When she had said that she had not been to my rooms during the afternoon, I had realized that any further questions would only result in repetitions of that statement. So I decided not to question her, at least not for the moment.

But what about the burnt papers? Should I not tell Uncle Josh? Dr. Harrison's warning rang in my ears—no undue excitement, no worry, a sick man. I decided that, in any case, I should discuss it with no one until I had completed the whole job once more. If I waited, I would be calmer and more rational. Moreover, whoever it was who had done this thing might be more likely to betray himself if I took no action. I felt that by adopting these tactics, I might stimulate my enemy's curiosity and thus, perhaps, find some clue to his or her identity.

Speculation was all very well, but it would not get the job done. I looked at the pile of ashes with something approaching nausea. I realized that I hated the sight of them, so I decided to get rid of them. I got down on my knees and carefully cleaned out the cupboard, putting the burnt papers onto the fire where their destruction was soon made total.

Once they were out of the way, I began to feel a little better; I was being illogical, I suppose, but the evil hand that had done this thing seemed further removed from me when the evidence of its infamy had been consumed.

So it was that I sat down at my desk and prepared, for the second time, to commence my task. As I fed the first sheet of paper into the machine, I thought, how different this is from Saturday, when I set to work for the first time. But it had to be done. At about eight o'clock, Barton brought me a tray of coffee and sandwiches and inquired solicitously about my health. Letty, it appeared, had told him that I was ill. He left after I had assured him that I was perfectly all right, that I did not need anything, and that all I wanted was to get on with my work undisturbed.

To my surprise, I found that I was really quite hungry, and I ate my sandwiches ravenously, though not without the foresight of putting two or three aside for later during what promised to be a long night. Feeling much better after I had eaten, I got back to work. The pile of typewritten sheets looked pathetically small and seemed to be taking an eternity to assume the satisfying bulk which would indicate that the job was well under way.

I do not remember how long it was after I had finished eating, a couple of hours I suspect, when I was interrupted by a tap on the door. I jumped; really, I was getting very nervous.

"Emma." It was Henry's voice on the other side of the door.

I went over and opened it. Henry walked into my sitting room.

"Hello, coz," he said. "What's all this I hear about you not being well?"

"Not well?" I replied. "Who told you that?"

"Actually, it was Barton. He said that you were indisposed, you know how he talks, and that you would not be down to dinner, so I thought the least a cousin could do was to come and find out if you needed anything.

"I'm afraid Barton must have got that from Letty," I replied. "I am quite all right, it's just . . . it's just that I have rather a lot of work to get through."

"But I thought that you had finished. Has that old scoundrel of a father of mine been laying it on too thick?" He said it lightly, but I could not help feeling that he really did mean to criticize Uncle Joshua.

"No," I replied. "He's been charming. I just haven't finished, and I still have quite a lot to go."

"Sorry, old girl," he said. "But I saw you out walking this afternoon and assumed that you must be finished."

"I wish that was true," I said.

"Look here, Emma," he said kindly. "I can't help thinking that there is something wrong. Wouldn't you like to tell me about it?"

"Yes, I would," I blurted out. I quickly corrected myself. "No, besides, there's nothing you could do." Suddenly I burst into tears.

He put an arm around me and murmured comforting things to me about being tired and overwrought. He led me to the sofa, where he sat me down ever so gently.

I was on the verge of telling him everything, for a trouble shared is a trouble halved. At that moment I was on the point of blurting out the whole story. I wanted, oh, how I wanted to. Why I did not I shall never know; it was as if something deep down inside of me forbade me to confide in him. Anyway, I said nothing.

"Would you like me to bring you a glass of brandy?" he asked.

"No, thank you," I replied. The moment had gone and I was again determined to keep to my original resolution and tell no one.

"Then at least let me pour you a cup of coffee," he said, going over to the pot and putting his hand on it. "Oh dear, it's stone cold. I'll have a fresh pot sent up to you."

"That would be nice," I replied. "Henry, I don't want to sound rude or ungrateful, but I do want to get on. Do you mind?"

"Of course not, coz," he smiled. "I'll be off." And as he got to the door, he said, "If you need anything, I'm two doors down on the other side of the corridor. Any time, day or night. And Emma. . . ."

"Yes," I replied as he paused.

"Be careful," he said, and he was gone.

Be careful? What did he mean by that? Was it a threat or a warning? Good heavens, I was really getting jumpy. I needed to take a firm grip on myself, or I was going to start seeing assassins behind every door and ghosts under every bed.

Once again I got back to the work at hand. Gradually the rhythm of the machine and my concentration on my task seemed to clear away the horrible thoughts which had been coursing through my mind. I was determined to finish in time. Above all, I knew that the one thing I could not allow myself to do was to let Uncle Joshua down. Although I knew that I could confide my fears in him alone, I also knew that this I would never do. Whatever I thought of her, whatever dark suspicions lurked in the back of my mind, Dr. Harrison had been right when she had warned me that Uncle Joshua was not to be worried or upset. He had known suffering and heartbreak enough. Probably the only thing that kept him going now was his work. In that, at least, I could help by shielding him from the knowledge of what had happened today. Whether the incident had been aimed at Uncle Joshua or myself, I did not know. I thought, on balance, that it was personally directed against me. If this was not so, why had the intruder made no apparent effort to find the original? There was, of course, always the possibility that he had gone about his or her loathsome task in such haste that he did not realize that the original was not with my typewriting. However, I could hardly believe this to be the case. No, I was almost sure that it had been me at whom he was aiming. This being so, I could see no advantage, even to myself, in discussing it with Uncle Joshua.

I had been working for about half an hour after Henry's departure when there was another tap on my door. Oh, I thought, that will be my fresh coffee. Henry had been most kind and thoughtful. I opened the door and found, to my surprise, that the bearer of my coffee tray was Dr. Harrison herself.

"May I step inside for a moment, Miss Waldron?" she asked in that flat, unemotional tone of voice which never seemed to vary.

"Well," I replied. "I really am very busy." The last person I wanted to see was Dr. Harrison, but she had been kind enough to bring up my tray and it would have been churlish to have refused her request. Quickly I corrected myself, fearing that she might think me rude. "I'm sorry, do come in for a little while. Perhaps you would care to join me in a cup of coffee?" I said, having observed that there were two cups on the tray.

She stepped inside, murmuring her thanks, and proceeded to pour out two cups of coffee. I sat down in one of the armchairs and sipped mine. The hot, bitter liquid tasted good, and I felt that I had been unkind to hesitate before asking her in. For a moment we sat in silence.

"Are you surprised that it is I who have brought your tray?" she asked.

"Well, yes, as a matter of fact I am," I replied.

This was quite true. The obvious thing for Henry to have done was either to bring it himself, or to send it up with one of the servants.

"I hope that you will not consider this an intrusion," she went on. "But Henry was most specific about my coming to see you. He said that he thought that you seemed a little distraught and that possibly you were feeling unwell."

I wished that Henry had not said that, though I could not condemn him, for he had shown only concern in telling the doctor that he was worried about me.

"No," I replied quite firmly. "I am not unwell. I have a great deal of work to get through before tomorrow evening, but as far as my health is concerned, I feel fine."

"You are quite sure?"

"Yes," I replied. "Quite sure."

"I would be most willing to examine you and prescribe some medication, should that be necessary, if you think that that might help at all?"

"No. That will not be necessary," I answered quickly.

Why did I feel repelled at the thought of this woman touching me? She was a doctor, and her attitude was very correct and professional. Had I met her in her consulting rooms I should, no doubt, have been most impressed by her cool, unemotional, efficient demeanor. But here in my own home, I could not stifle the feeling of revulsion which welled up within me.

"Very well, Miss Waldron. We'll say no more about it at the moment, but please do not hesitate to call on me should you ever require my services professionally," she said. And then, changing the subject, she continued, "By the way, I have not had the opportunity of seeing you alone since our talk on Saturday. Have you given any thought to what I said then?"

I was relieved at the chance of giving her a frank and honest reply.

"Why, yes," I said. "I have given the matter a great deal of thought, and you may rest assured that I shall do my best to follow your advice and do nothing knowingly which will cause my uncle any distress."

"Thank you, Miss Waldron, I find myself much relieved," she replied. "Well, I shall not detain you any longer, as you say that you have work to do. I have to look in on your uncle before I retire, so I shall bid you goodnight." And she was gone.

I returned to my work. Gradually, as the hours wore on, stillness came upon the house. Not that stillness which one experiences from being alone in one's room, but the deep, heavy silence which pervades when a large house has gone to sleep. All the little noises of the day which had passed unnoticed were now recognizable in their absence. This was the deep velvet silence of all familiar things sleeping, unconscious of the other sounds which had taken their place. Every noise was magnified a hundredfold by the heavy silence of the night: the minute patter of small feet somewhere in the rafters as some small creature scurried about its nocturnal business, the occasional hoot of an owl and the lowing of a restless beast in the fields.

I had never before worked through a whole night, and I found, much to my surprise, that the experience was, far from being scary, in fact comforting. Only once during the dark hours did I get a fright and that only momentary; it was when a vixen, somewhere out on the moor, gave forth a shrill cry which sounded just like a baby in agony. This apart, the whole atmosphere I found most conducive to my work.

Luckily, I had been left with a full scuttle of coal, so I was able to keep my fire well-stoked. The flames were warm and friendly as they danced away. They were thrown into bold relief by the black fire wall behind them.

As I ploughed through the papers and the pile of completed sheets grew, I got to thinking again about the deliberate destruction of my first effort. Up to now I had allowed my suspicions to fall only upon those people with whom I had had immediate contact: Henry, Dr. Harrison, Roger, and Letty. As I mentally reviewed the situation with a little more objectivity, I realized that there were several other possibilities. There were several other servants in the house, three of whom I had never met before. As I could not think of any really valid reason for an attack upon me personally, even though the facts might seem to point in that direction, I began to speculate elsewhere.

Remembering the warning which I had received about secrecy, was it not possible that someone had been planted in the house with the deliberate intention of sabotaging the whole Kittiwake project? Accepting this as a possibility, it could be any one of the servants and most likely one who had joined the household within recent months. I made a mental resolution to check with Barton as to when he had engaged all of the people who had not been at Goathlands at the time of my departure eight years ago. If there proved to be one who had been engaged during recent months, I could at least check their references without raising suspicion.

What should I do if I found that someone had, for example, secured a post at Goathlands on forged references? I could, of course, dismiss them instantly, but that might not be an altogether good idea. To know your enemy is a great advantage, but to make him aware of your knowledge is to nullify any advantage there might be.

One fact, not altogether to my liking, was beginning to emerge. The person with whom I should have to share my suspicions was the insufferable Roger. He was the one person who had nothing to gain by spoiling the plans for Kittiwake or, even if he had, with his intimate knowledge of the project, he could have handled it in a much more efficient way and without raising any suspicion. Reluctantly, I came to the conclusion that this was indeed so, and that Roger it would have to be.

Bearing this in mind, I determined to try and break the ice with him during the next few days. I certainly did not want to have anything to do with him personally; nothing could be further from my thoughts, I insisted to myself. However, because he was to be my confidante and ally, it would help if we were on speaking terms.

A bird started to sing away in the distance, and then another. Dawn was here. The sounds of the night had vanished away as imperceptibly as they had started. I drew back the curtains and looked out over the moors to the east, where the first streaks of crimson were appearing on the horizon. There had been a slight frost during the night, and the silver moors sparkled and glistened as the great golden orb of the sun climbed slowly over the horizon and consumed them with its first warming rays.

I was by then well over halfway through my task, and the thought that I would finish it on time stimulated me and banished the sleepiness which was, by then, attempting to possess me. I paused just long enough to enjoy the beauty of the sunrise, and then went back to work.

The night was over, and with the coming of the dawn I had made my resolutions. My plan of action was now clear. I should not be parted from my work until it was completed and safely in Uncle Joshua's hand. I did not intend to take any unnecessary risks. I would then rest until dinner. As soon as the opportunity should arise, I would discuss the whole of the happenings of the previous twenty-four hours with Roger.

Promptly at eight o'clock the door opened and Letty came in with my morning tea. I was on the point of reproving her for not knocking when I realized that she would naturally expect to find me still in bed.

"Oh, you're up, miss," she said, somewhat surprised. "Would you like to take your tea in here?"

"Good morning, Letty," I replied. "Yes, I'll have it here."

She put the tray down and headed for the bedroom.

"Where are you going?" I asked as she opened the door.

"I was going to . . . oh, you've done your own bed, miss," she said in an astonished voice.

"Letty, I have been making my own bed for eight years," I replied, not wishing to lie, but equally not wanting her to know that it had not been slept in.

"Don't you like the way I do it, miss?" She sounded worried.

"Of course I do. You make my bed beautifully," I replied. "Please think no more about it, and you can take these things away now." I indicated the now rather sordid-looking remains of my coffee.

"Yes, miss," she said, and started to gather them up.

"And Letty, you can bring me up lots of bacon and eggs, toast, and marmalade at about nine o'clock."

"Yes, miss, tea or coffee, miss?"

"Coffee," I replied. "Strong coffee."

Letty left me. As I sipped the tea and nibbled at the biscuits that Letty had brought, I realized that I was very hungry, and I found myself wishing that I had asked for my breakfast to be served immediately. I drank two cups of tea, and after carefully locking the door to the corridor, I permitted myself the luxury of a hot bath.

I dried myself and put on clean clothes, and feeling very much better, I returned to the sitting room and unlocked the door just in time for Letty to bring in my breakfast.

"You've changed your clothes, miss," she said as she put the tray down.

"Yes, Letty," I replied. Bother the girl. Was she prying, or did she consider it her duty to comment on everything that she saw?

"Do you want anything else, miss?"

"No, Letty, you can leave everything until lunch time," I replied.

Letty left me. I tucked into my breakfast and then went back to my work. By noon I had finished, and I murmured a little prayer of thanks that I had been able to complete the job on time. Once again, I carefully collated the papers and put them into their manilla folders. Then, armed with my labors, I set off in the direction of Uncle Joshua's room.

I saw no one as I walked through the house; I supposed that everyone must be about his or her business. As I approached Uncle Joshua's room I noticed that the door was ajar. As I got nearer, I was surprised to hear the sound of angry voices raised in heated argument. I could not make out what was being said in any detail, but I got the impression that the argument was about money. I hesitated, clutching my precious bundle. Should I just walk in or should I leave and return in an hour or so?

The question was answered for me when suddenly the door was flung wide and Henry stormed out. His face was blazing with anger as he strode straight past me. I do not think that he was even aware of my presence as I stood with my back pressed against the wall. His expression was really most frightening. His normally calm, handsome face was flushed and twisted in anger, he was breathing heavily, and his fists were clenched so tightly that his knuckles shone white against his skin.

When he had passed, I hesitantly went through the now wide-open door and to my horror saw that Uncle Josh was sitting, half lying, slumped in his chair, his poor handless arm thumping away at his breast, while his mouth opened and closed as great choking gasps came from him as if he were having difficulty in drawing breath.

"Uncle Josh," I cried as I ran towards him. "Uncle Josh, are you all right?"

He made no reply. I do not think that he even heard me. I realized immediately what I must do. I must get Dr. Harrison to him as quickly as possible. I flew to the door, intending to rush across the corridor and call her, but as I reached the door, she was there.

She pushed past me and went directly to Uncle Joshua. "Go to my room and get my bag. It's on the table by the window," she snapped.

"Is he . . ." I started to ask if he was going to be all right.

"Don't stand there, do what I say," she said, interrupting me.

I rushed across the corridor and into her room. There, as she had said, by the window was her black medical bag. I grabbed it and hurried back to her.

She was bending over Uncle Joshua, having loosened his collar and tie, as I took the bag to her.

"Give it to me," she said.

"Is there anything I can do?" I asked.

"Do?" she said as she opened her bag. When she looked up at me, there was anger, almost hatred, in her face. "Don't you think that you have done enough? Is this how you keep your promise to shield him from worry and emotion?" She transferred her glare to the papers I was still holding. "Get out of here and take that rubbish with you."

Chapter Seven

I WENT OUT into the corridor. I was desperately worried about Uncle Joshua but absolutely furious that that woman could be so stupid as to think that I was responsible for his present condition. More than anything, I wanted to find out whether my uncle's condition was serious, but I dared not go back into that room. Moreover, I still had the papers. Oh, how I wanted to be rid of them. "Rubbish" she had called them. Did she know what they contained? Did she perhaps know and disapprove? Disapprove so strongly that she could be the one who had reduced my first efforts to ashes? The question was hammering at my brain. Maybe she thought that this concentration on his work was bad for Uncle Joshua. But even if she believed that, she was not going to ease the situation by making his work more difficult. As for her accusing me, I had to admit that in the heat of the moment she could have assumed that I was responsible. After all, when she had entered the room, I had been alone with Uncle Josh. Even so, she could have asked me what had happened; my reply might even have proved of some help in her treatment of him.

I was calmer now and realized that I could accomplish nothing by standing outside Uncle Joshua's door, clutching my papers and wondering and worrying about what was happening inside the room. For better or for worse,

Uncle Joshua had to be left in Dr. Harrison's hands. But what about the papers? I had to get rid of them; they were like a millstone around my neck. Every moment that they were in my possession I was terrified that something might happen to them. I decided that I must hand them over to Roger. He had been present when I had received my instructions and was obviously aware of their contents. I made up my mind that I would tell him that Uncle Joshua was unwell but would keep the actual circumstances to myself.

Having made up my mind as to my course of action, I left the house and headed toward the big barn. When I arrived there, the small door was closed but unlocked. I opened it.

"Roger," I called.

There was a low growl.

"Stay, Basil," said Roger's voice. "Who's there?" he shouted.

"It's me, Emma," I replied.

"All right, stay there and I'll come over," he called.

I waited at the door until he stepped outside, his eyes blinking in the glare of the sunlight.

"Well, if it isn't Miss Waldron," he said. "And what can I do for you?"

"I want to deliver these to you," I said, offering him the papers.

"Is that the typewriting?" he asked. "But I thought you were supposed to deliver them to your uncle."

"At the moment my uncle is not very well," I answered. "I thought that as he had asked for them to be delivered by this time today I had better let you have them."

"Not well? He's been overdoing it again, you know. All right, I'll take them over to him."

It was with a feeling of great relief that I finally handed him the papers.

"I don't know if it makes any difference," I said as he took them from me. "But Dr. Harrison is with him just now, or was until a minute or so ago."

"Oh," he replied. "In that case I'll take them over later. If that old dragon has got him in her clutches she won't let anyone near him." He smiled at me.

He had such a nice smile, it made me feel all warm and toasty inside. I found it hard to remember that this was the man who had been so rude to me.

"Mr. Attwood . . ." I began.

"Why don't you call me Roger?" he said.

"I wouldn't dream of doing any such thing," I replied haughtily.

"Oh, yes you would, you know," he said. "As a matter of fact, you've already done it."

"I have done no such thing," I retorted indignantly. "When did I call you Roger? I don't believe it."

"When you called me from the door."

"I . . ." Oh dear, it was true. I had called him by his first name, though it was very rude of him to remind me.

"You see, you remember."

He was becoming insufferable again, but it was a small point and I had resolved to enlist his aid.

"Very well, since it seems to be important to you I shall do as you ask," I said, in the tone one uses when humoring a persistent child. "But you need not think that I approve of this sort of familiarity."

"I would never dream of it." He was mocking me. "And you can rest assured that I shall never refer to you as Emma unless you give me your express permission, Emma."

"You are so rude," I said.

"All right, Your Highness, forgive me, I'm sorry. I tell you what I'll do, I'll show her to you."

"You'll show whom to me?" I demanded.

"The woman I love." Before I could reply, he added, "I'm talking about Kittiwake. After all, you are one of the team now, so I see no reason why you should not be allowed to look at her. She's going to fly tomorrow and everybody will see her."

I was curious; who wouldn't be? So I allowed him to lead me into the big barn and down to the far end where his beloved stood.

"There," he said. "Isn't she beautiful?"

They say that beauty is in the eye of the beholder. If this is true, then he and I were seeing two very different things. Before me stood a flimsy, gawky, spindle-shanked contrivance with a black ugly mass of engine at the front. It was a mass of wires and open spaces and it was without doubt one of the most evil-smelling objects I have ever seen. I looked at him to see if he had been joking, but no, there was an expression of rapture on his face as he gazed at that monstrosity. Surely he did not intend to risk his life by trying to fly in that.

"You're not really going to fly it, are you?" I asked.

"Fly it?" he replied. "Of course I'm going to fly it, and it is going to be the most wonderful experience of my life."

"Have you ever flown anything before?"

"To be perfectly honest, Emma," he paused, "no."

He was quite mad. I was sure of it.

"You see," he continued, "there are so few flying machines, if you want to fly, the only way to do it is to build one for yourself and simply fly it. Of course I have been lucky. I have had your uncle. Sir Joshua has one of the finest engineering brains I have ever met. Every detail has been worked out on the drawing board so that, though neither I nor Kittiwake have ever flown before, both of us know exactly what the other is going to do up there tomorrow." He gazed affectionately at the contraption. "And now I'm hungry. Coming to lunch?"

His question brought me to the realization of how tired I was. I was sure that I could not face lunch, and with the dinner party that evening, if I was to be any sort of a hostess at all I simply had to get some rest.

"Thank you, but I think I shall miss lunch," I replied. "I've been working very hard these last few days and must get some rest. You could do me a favor, though, and ask Barton if he would deal with the arrangements for dinner and send a pot of tea up to my room at five o'clock."

Roger agreed to do as I had asked and I went up to my room. How strange, I thought; there had been a perfect opportunity to tell him about the burnt papers but for some reason the thought had never entered my head.

I got to my room and stretched out on my bed. I kicked my shoes off but found that I did not even have the energy to undress.

It seemed that I had no sooner closed my eyes than I heard Letty's voice.

"It's five o'clock, miss."

I rubbed my eyes. I felt awful. My tongue seemed like a lump of dried flannel in my mouth. I sat up.

"It can't be five o'clock already," I complained.

"It is, miss, I've put your tea in the sitting room. Would you rather have it in here, miss?"

"No thank you, Letty, leave it where it is," I replied.

"Yes, miss. What are you going to wear tonight, miss?"

The last thing I wanted just then was to get into a conversation with Letty, or with anybody, for that matter.

"Just leave everything, Letty," I said. "I will sort my own clothes out."

"What about your room, miss, I haven't done it yet."

Oh dear, I could not be unkind to the girl. She really was most willing and I was aware that the strain of the last days had caused me to be very short with her.

"Letty, I hope you don't mind," I said. "I just want to

be alone. I wonder if you would be so kind as to do me a really great favor and do my room while we are at dinner. I would really appreciate that."

"Oh, yes, miss, of course, miss. I'll leave you right away and come up after you have gone down to dinner."

"Thank you, Letty. Have the guests arrived yet?"

"Yes, miss, they're with Sir Joshua."

That was good news, anyway; it meant that Uncle Josh was all right.

"Thank you for being so patient with me, Letty, you're a good girl. You can leave me now."

I felt a little more human after I had drunk two cups of tea and washed in cold water. My wardrobe was not extensive and it contained none of the then fashionable hobble-skirted gowns. Not that I regarded this as a tragedy. The hobble skirt was one of those strange garments which women occasionally allow the fashion dictators to foist upon them with no regard for personal comfort. I never owned one and never would. I chose a gown of pink satin velvet with a tailored, tight waisted bodice and leg of mutton sleeves worn over a beautiful old modesty vest trimmed with Brussels lace.

I did my hair and dressed. Really, life would have been much easier had I had Letty to assist me. Dressing for a formal occasion was a two-handed job, but I managed it. The result, when I observed myself in the long mirror, was very pleasing.

Dinner was at seven-thirty for eight o'clock, so at seven-twenty-five I went down to the withdrawing room, where I found Henry waiting, looking very elegant in his evening dress.

"Hello, coz," he said. "Glad you made it. I say, you look an absolute stunner."

It was the same rather flippant Henry, giving no indication of the incident earlier in the day or whether or not he had seen me in the corridor when he stormed past. I wondered if, in fact, he knew that his father had been ill. He pulled out his watch.

"They'll be here soon," he said. "Can I get you a glass of sherry before they arrive?"

"No, thank you," I replied. As I have explained, I did not drink at all, though I was aware that, for the sake of politeness, I should have to take a little wine with my meal that evening.

Roger, Dr. Harrison, and our four guests, resplendent in their regimental evening dress, arrived during the next few minutes. Fortunately, Roger was the first to arrive, so he was able to make the necessary introductions while Henry poured sherry for our guests. At that time I did not get a chance to speak to Dr. Harrison, so I had no means of knowing whether or not she still regarded me as responsible for the condition in which she had found Uncle Joshua that morning. As always on such occasions, the conversation was trivial.

Promptly at eight o'clock, Barton opened the double doors leading on to the dining room and announced that dinner was served. One of our guests, a Colonel Willoughby, approached me.

"Pardon me, ma'am," he said. "As senior officer present, may I claim the privilege of taking you into dinner?" His voice sounded as if it would be much more at home on a barrack square than in a drawing room.

"Thank you, Colonel," I replied, as he gallantly offered me his arm. "I would be honored."

The polished mahogany table looked beautiful with its two flickering candelabra, which made the Georgian silver place settings sparkle against their dark background. The meal was served quietly and efficiently by Barton and his staff. The conversation centered mainly around flying machines, and I was quite surprised to find how much of it made sense to me, as a result, no doubt, of my labors of the last few days. Colonel Willoughby was most charming and courteous and attempted several times to draw me into the conversation. However, I did not wish to air my knowledge and I was still feeling somewhat fatigued, so I spent most of the meal, as indeed every good hostess should, listening attentively and seeing that my guests were provided for.

As the meal drew to a close I rose and, speaking to Dr. Harrison for the first time, suggested that we withdraw and leave the gentlemen to their port wine and cigars. Coffee was awaiting us in the withdrawing room, and as I poured out two cups in silence, I wondered what on earth I was going to say to her. It was, however, Dr. Harrison who broke the silence and she did so in a most unexpected and welcome manner.

"Miss Waldron," she said hesitantly.

"Yes," I answered, wondering what could be coming.

"Miss Waldron, I feel that I owe you an apology. Sir Joshua has acquainted me with the facts about this morning and I realize that I was wrong to speak to you in the manner in which I did. The only excuse I can offer is that I was extremely worried about my patient and very angry that he should have been brought to that condition. Please forgive me."

Under the circumstances, it was a very gracious apology. I felt I could not in conscience be less gracious in reply.

"Please, doctor," I said, "think no more about it, I am quite aware that it was concern for my uncle that caused you to say what you did, and I should hate to think that you would reprove yourself on that count. As it happens, I had only just entered the room and was on my way to call you when you came in. What is much more important, and I know that you will agree, is how my uncle is now."

"He is as well as he ever will be," she replied. "What is most vital is to do all we can to see that nothing is done which could bring about any more of these attacks."

So it was all right. Uncle Josh was well and I was no longer suspected. I wondered if Uncle Josh had told Dr. Harrison that it was Henry, but as she did not volunteer any information in that direction, I did not pursue the point. Our conversation retrogressed into small talk of little or no consequence. Dr. Harrison, having made her apology, resumed her attitude of stoicism, and I was really quite relieved when the gentlemen had finished their cigars and joined us.

As soon as it was polite to do so, I made my farewells and retired. Kittiwake was to fly the following morning at nine, and I wanted to get a good night's sleep before that. I went upstairs, undressed, and fell into bed. I think I was asleep as soon as my head hit the pillow.

The following morning, Letty brought me my tea a little earlier than usual. She was in a state of great excitement. She told me that the servants had been informed of the impending flight and that Mr. Barton had obtained permission from Uncle Joshua for them all to go out onto the west lawn and witness the event.

The west lawn covered a very large area about three acres in all. When I got there, having finished breakfast at about a quarter to nine, I found our military friends had already arrived. But as they seemed to be deep in conversation with Roger, I did not approach them.

Barton, ever the despot below stairs, had taken command of his staff and had had benches brought out for them to sit on. They were assembling to the accompaniment of a great deal of noisy chatter. I noticed Letty among them, and I smiled at her when she caught my eye. To this she responded with a pert bob, obviously showing off to the two junior footmen who seemed to be vying for her attention. I glanced up at the house, and there I could see Uncle Joshua sitting at the window of his room with Dr. Harrison standing by his side. I waved up to him and he waved back to me. It seemed to be a very happy and excited gathering.

Suddenly a cheer went up from where the servants were sitting and looking over toward the big barn, now standing with its massive doors wide open, I saw Kittiwake emerge, being pushed by Ormerod and our two grooms, one of whom was holding the tail end off the ground. I was watching this, thinking that it looked even more fragile than it had done in the barn, when a voice behind me spoke.

"Well, aren't you going to wish us luck?"

It was Roger. He was dressed in a black leather jacket and wore a tight-fitting helmet of the same material. Pushed up over his brow was an enormous pair of goggles.

"Of course I am," I replied. "Good luck, Roger." Then I did an incredible thing, for which I can only plead the excitement of the moment. I kissed him lightly on the cheek.

I could feel the color rushing to my face. How could I have done such a thing? I was embarrassed and confused.

"Thanks, I shall never shave again," he said, smiling flippantly.

I felt dreadful. After all, I hardly knew the man, and most of what I did know I found quite objectionable.

"I do beg your pardon," I said.

"Please don't apologize," he replied, laughing. "I enjoyed it."

The brute. He was obviously no gentleman, and I was about to tell him so, but he turned away and headed for his flying contraption, which by then Ormerod and his stalwarts had rolled to the far end of the lawn.

Colonel Willoughby approached me.

"Pardon me, Miss Waldron, but you seem to be alone here, and I wondered whether you would care to come and join us?"

"How kind of you to ask," I replied. "But if you will excuse me, I think I would rather stay where I am." I don't know why it was, but I wanted to be alone.

"Just as you wish, ma'am," said the Colonel. "I think you might find these useful."

He offered me an enormous pair of field glasses.

"Oh, but I couldn't, what are you going to do?" I really believe that, as a class, our British Army officers are the most generous and thoughtful people in the world.

"Always prepared for an emergency, got a spare pair, you know."

Colonel Willoughby left me. I put the glasses to my eyes and focused them carefully on Kittiwake. Roger had reached it by that time and was deep in conversation with Ormerod. Roger went to the cockpit and leaned inside of it for a few moments while Ormerod took up position just in front of the tail. The two grooms stood just in front of the wing on either side of the machine. They were both holding pieces of rope, each of which was attached to a triangular block of wood placed in front of each wheel. Roger came round to the front of the machine and seized hold of the propeller. He swung the propeller about four times, stepping back and away from it each time he did so. Then he went back and again leaned into the cockpit.

There was a buzz of conversation and a giggle or two from where the servants were sitting and I heard a sharp word of reproof from Barton. They presumably thought that there was something wrong and that Kittiwake would not go. It gave me a sense of superiority to feel that I was probably the only lay person present who knew, albeit from my typewriting, that it was not supposed to go quite yet. The purpose of the first swings had been to draw fuel into the engine. Now, after Roger had switched on something called the magneto, the engine should start.

Roger was back at the propeller. He gave a signal to

Ormerod, who laid himself across the body, just in front of the tail. Then Roger took hold of the tip of the propeller and swung it downwards, again stepping away as he did this. It was well that he did, for this time, with a clatter and a bang and a large puff of smoke, the engine roared into life and the propeller disappeared into a whirling disk. Roger then ran around the wing and clambered into the cockpit, where he sat, now visible from only just above the waist. He pulled down his goggles and pulled up a scarf over his mouth, thus becoming completely unrecognizable. He leaned forward and did something which resulted in the roar of the motor increasing. Poor Ormerod, lying across the rear end and being shaken near to death I should think, lost his hat.

Roger slowed the engine down and then raised his arm and waved it from side to side. Ormerod, who had his head turned in Roger's direction, saw the signal and heaved himself off the tail while the two grooms, conscious that all eyes were upon them, pulled away the wooden blocks and ran behind the machine to join Ormerod.

For a little while the only movement was the waggling of the rudder and the other moving parts which were on the wings and tail. Then Roger leaned forward, the engine noise rose to a crescendo, and slowly the Kittiwake started to roll forward across the lawn. Faster and faster it moved. First the tail lifted off the ground, and then the wheels bounced up and down again. I held my breath as they came off the ground again, but this time it was the real thing. Slowly the gap between Kittiwake and the lawn increased, a foot, ten feet, twenty feet, until it must have been a hundred feet. A great cheer went up from all of us. Kittiwake was flying.

As I watched I thought how strange it was that this machine, which had looked so awkward and fragile standing on the ground, was now, now that it had entered the element for which it had been designed, a thing of grace and beauty. I peered through my field glasses and watched Roger as he turned the machine and headed toward us. How we all gasped as he swooped low over the lawn at an incredible speed. Someone said later that he must have been going at fifty miles an hour, though I found that a little hard to credit.

Three or four times Kittiwake flew across the lawn. Finally it turned, far away to the right of us. As it came toward us, getting lower and lower, the engine was coughing and spluttering, in marked contrast to the steady roar which it had made before. Lower and lower, slower and slower it came until finally it touched down on the lawn. As it did this, Ormerod and the grooms rushed toward it and grabbed hold of the tips of the wings. The engine stopped, the propeller was still, and everyone cheered and ran towards Kittiwake, the servants heedless of Barton's remonstrations.

I was the only one who did not move. I stood where I was, thankful that all was well, that Roger was safe and that Uncle Joshua had had his triumph.

I looked up at the house, and there was Uncle Joshua, waving away with his good arm, though to whom I do not know, for apart from myself, everyone was clustered round Kittiwake. They were slapping Roger on the back and cheering. Up there in the house beside Uncle Josh, Dr. Harrison stood impassive and unsmiling as ever. I felt that I must go to him. After all, this was really his day. So without more ado, I went into the house and up to his room.

Uncle Joshua was delighted. He looked happier than I have ever seen him either before or since. Even Dr. Harrison announced gravely that it had been a most satisfactory morning. We looked out of the window as Kittiwake, under the watchful eye of Roger, was trundled back into the big barn. As the huge doors swung shut, Uncle Josh turned to me.

"Well, my dear," he said. "You've done a great job. There was nothing but praise for your typewriting and for your charm as a hostess. I do so hope that you will never ever consider leaving Goathlands again. I want you to be happy here and to feel that this house is every bit as much your home as it was when your dear parents were alive. Promise me that you will stay."

The success of Kittiwake and the infectious joy of Uncle Joshua had acted on me like a heady wine. All the dark thoughts and worries of the previous days had vanished from my mind. I was happy at Goathlands. Here I was surrounded by well-loved things, familiar since childhood. Most important was Uncle Josh himself, who so obviously loved me and wanted me to stay.

"I promise," I said, and I meant it. "But what about Henry? After all, Goathlands will be his one day, what does he think?"

"I'm glad you asked me that," said Uncle Josh. "As you know, Henry and I do not always get on well together. In this, however, we are in one accord. It was, you may be surprised to learn, he who first suggested that I try and get you to come and stay with us. Nothing to do with the typewriting, of course, he did not know about that. I think that in his peculiar way he is rather fond of you."

The mention of Henry reminded me that I had not noticed him on the lawn during the flight. I mentioned this to Uncle Josh.

"Well, you know Henry," he replied. "He was never interested in Kittiwake, and he told me that he had a long-standing appointment in Whitby this morning. He'll be back in time for luncheon and to say farewell to our guests. But let us not bother about that. What are you going to do for the rest of the day?"

"I," I said, coming to a sudden decision, "am going to take Honey out for a good stiff gallop across the moors as soon as our guests have gone."

"Good idea," said Uncle Joshua. "How I wish I could come with you."

Before I could reply, Dr. Harrison interrupted.

"Sir Joshua, I know Miss Waldron will not mind, but I am going to ask her to leave now. You have had enough excitement this morning to last you a week. You must rest now."

"Of course, doctor," I said. "Goodbye, uncle, I'll come and see you again tomorrow morning."

"Goodbye, my dear, give Honey an extra sugar lump from me. I'm sorry you can't stay, but you see how she bullies me."

I left them. As I made my way to my room, I was feeling happy and contented. I would change before lunch, bid our guests farewell, and then take Honey out. I got to my room and rang for Letty. I told her to tell one of the grooms to have Honey ready for me at half past two.

Strange, I thought, that Henry should have been the one to suggest that I come to Goathlands. Whenever I had contacted him he had assured me that my presence here was unnecessary. I supposed he must have had a change of mind.

I went to my window and looked out.

It was a lovely day.

Chapter Eight

LUNCH WAS TO be at one, so, as I had plenty of time, I decided to change and get ready for my outing before going down to lunch. My riding habit was in fine black broadcloth, and I wore it over a heavy silk blouse that had an attached stock. After I had dressed, I stood for a moment and admired myself in the mirror. I have always felt that a riding habit is one of the most flattering outfits that a woman can ever wear.

On my way down to lunch I met Henry in the hall.

"Hello, coz," he greeted me. "Have you been riding?"

"Not yet, Henry," I replied. "I'm not going out until two-thirty. Have you just got back?"

"Yes," he replied. "I'm sorry I was not able to be here for the circus this morning. How did everything go?"

"Wonderfully, it was a great success," I answered. "Are you coming in to lunch?"

"No thank you, I had a snack in Whitby," he said. "I would like to come up and have afternoon tea with you, if you don't mind. We don't seem to have had the chance for a chat since you arrived."

"That would be nice," I replied. "Why don't you tell Letty that you will be coming."

"Thanks, coz, I'll do that," said Henry.

I left him and headed toward the dining room.

Roger did not appear at luncheon. I supposed that he must have had a lot to do checking over Kittiwake after his triumph that morning, so I told Barton to arrange a packed lunch and send it over to the big barn. I was beginning to feel quite at home as mistress of Goathlands, and I was really enjoying the experience.

After lunch, a groom brought one of Uncle Joshua's horseless carriages to the front door. Barton, with his usual efficiency, had arranged this. I was in the process of saying goodbye to our guests when I suddenly remembered that I had forgotten to return the field glasses to Colonel Willoughby. I asked him to wait while I sent for them but, charming man that he was, he insisted that I regard them as a hostess present and keep them for myself.

I stood on the front steps and waved farewell as the noisy machine clattered and spluttered down the drive.

Then I went inside. As I went upstairs the clock in the entrance hall was just chiming a quarter past two. I hurried to my rooms and put on my boots and riding topper. I got my riding whip from the wardrobe. Of course I never beat my horse, but it is impossible to ride sidesaddle without a whip. It fulfills the same functions as are performed by a gentleman's right leg when riding astride, and without a whip you could never steer your mount.

Ready at last, I went out of the house and headed toward the stables by way of the big barn. In the barn I found a somewhat greasy Roger sitting on a box, eating a sandwich, and gazing adoringly at Kittiwake. He rose to his feet as he caught sight of me.

"Thanks for the lunch. I'd forgotten all about it," he said. "My goodness, you do look smart."

"Thank you," I replied.

"Ormerod told me that you were going to take Honey out," he went on. "Take care, I gather he hasn't had very much work lately."

"I'll be careful," I said. Then, changing the subject, I said, "Congratulations on this morning."

His concern had made me feel warm and cozy inside. Why, I asked myself, should I find this man so attractive and so irritating at one and the same time?

"I did very little, really," he said. "All the difficult work was done by Sir Joshua. Anyone could have done my part, even you." He chuckled.

There, he had spoiled it again; he did not seem able to resist these little witticisms. I said goodbye and left him standing there, a sandwich in one hand, a spanner in the other, and grease all over his overalls.

I found Ormerod waiting for me when I got to the stables.

"Honey's all ready for thee, miss," he said. "He's in the loose box. Shall I get him for thee?"

"No thank you, Ormerod, I'll get him myself."

"Then thou'll be needing this," he said, handing me an apple. "Where do thou fancy going?"

It was not just idle curiosity. If ever anyone took a horse out, Ormerod always wanted to know their intended route so that in the event of an accident he would know where to look for them.

"I'll take him down Howl Moor to Wheeldale Beck and then ride clockwise round the boundary. I might try a jump or two over Blawath Beck." I smiled, knowing that he would caution me.

"Well, thou be careful if thou are going to do any jumping, Miss Emma. He's had very little work for long enough. I'd sweat him a bit before I'd try jumping him if I was thee."

"Don't worry, Ormerod," I said, smiling again. "I'm not going to take any risks."

"I hope not, Miss Emma, but I've heard thee say things like that before. Thou's a gradely horsewoman but I reckon that thou's as much out of practice as Honey."

"I promise I'll be good," I said.

I went into Honey's loose box. He was standing there tacked up and ready. As soon as he saw me, he nuzzled me and started to sniff around for the apple. I gave it to him, and he was munching away at it as I led him out.

"Shall I check the girth?" Ormerod was not really offering, he was reminding me. One of the first lessons I ever learned about horsemanship was that you never leave your girth to anyone else, but you always check it yourself. I lifted up the saddle flap and pulled the girth leathers up another hole.

"Ready, miss?"

I nodded. He made a stirrup with his hands, and I put my foot into it. Then, with no effort at all, he lifted me into the saddle.

As soon as Honey felt my weight he started to dance. Gently I pulled the reins, talking to him all the time. In a moment or two he was standing still, though he was still tossing his head.

"I told thee he was fresh," said Ormerod. "I should take him into the paddock for ten minutes first, and then if he's still tossing about I'll slip a martingale on him."

Ormerod was right, of course; he always was about anything to do with horses. A little schooling first, before we went out, would be a good thing for both of us.

The gate of the paddock was open, as there were no other horses out at that time, so I walked Honey in and started him circling. He behaved magnificently. I walked, trotted and cantered him, first to the right and then to the left. Then I cantered a few figure eights to see whether he would change his lead leg as we changed from the right to the left hand circle. Honey was absolutely perfect. When I came to the final test and asked him to stand, he stood stock still. It was like the old days all over again. I could feel the powerful beast beneath me, excited and wanting to be off but all the time waiting for the command, the pressure of leg or whip or the gentle tug on his mouth.

"Thou'll do," said Ormerod, who had been leaning over the fence and watching us critically. "Take him out now and give him a bit of work."

We turned out of the paddock and set off at a slow trot down Howl Moor. The land starts to fall away quite rapidly not far from the house, so we slowed to a walk until we arrived at Wheeldale Beck. I then turned north and headed at a gentle hand canter along the bank of the stream. We arrived at Nelly Ayre Fosse after about a mile. Who Nelly Ayre was, I have no idea, but a fosse is a ditch, and I must say that I was tempted to try a couple of jumps there. But remembering Ormerod's warning and knowing that he had been right, I decided that Honey had better have a good gallop first. So it was that I turned Honey towards an old Celtic burial ground which lay about two miles to the east over fairly flat country.

I let Honey have his head. He stretched out and swept over the ground in long effortless strides. My father always used to say that the finest sight in the world was a stretch of open country seen over the top of a horse's head. There was no country more beautiful than the Yorkshire moors, and no horse quite so fine as Honey. Within about five or six minutes we had arrived at the two mounds which were our destination, and I reined him in gently. He fought for his head, and it was a little while before I could get him to stand. Even then, he was tossing his head and pawing at the ground with his right forefoot. However, even this stopped after I had talked to him a little. Once he had completely calmed down, we set off again at a walk. He was sweating a little around the neck, but it was nothing much; he was obviously in very good condition. Every now and then he would pull at his bit, indicating that he wanted to be off again, but I had decided that I would cool him down a bit first before trying anything energetic.

We went south as far as Northdale Scar, walking slowly below the cliff which climbed away toward Crag Stone Rigg. Then, walking all the while, we turned east toward Blawath Beck. I rode Honey into the stream, and though he hesitated a little at first, he was soon enjoying himself, splashing his way through the water. After a hundred yards or so, I took him out onto the far bank and continued downstream. On my left was a thick wood, the north end of Pickering Forest, now turning brown and scarlet and gold as the autumn hues took over from summer. To my right, standing on top of Two Howes Rigg, I could see Goathlands, now glowing pink in the afternoon sunshine.

I knew the spot for which I was looking. I had known it since childhood and I succeeded in finding it with very little difficulty. It was a point at which the stream was about ten or twelve feet wide, with a wide grassy bank on either side. I stopped and walked Honey to the water's edge in order to let him have a look at the jump.

"Do you think you can still jump it, Honeybunch?" I asked him, patting his neck.

I turned and trotted him away from the stream and at about thirty yards, swung him round to face the stream once more. Horses either love to jump or else they hate it and will never jump. Honey was one of those who loved jumping, and as I turned him I knew that he had got the idea. His ears pricked and his body all aquiver, he was pulling hard at the bit and wanting to be off.

I touched him with my whip and let him have his head. He needed no further encouragement but jumped off immediately into a gallop. The stream was rushing toward us, I felt him gathering himself for the leap and then rising to the jump, and then I started to swing my body backwards for the landing. . . .

Everything went black.

Chapter Nine

I HAVE NO idea how long I lay there, though I suppose it could not have been for more than a minute or two. When I came to, I was lying on the north bank of the stream, half in and half out of the water. I was in a very dazed condition and quite unable to focus my eyes on any object. It was with great difficulty that I dragged myself two or three feet up the bank so that I was clear of the water.

For a few minutes I sat there on the bank, holding my head in my hands and waiting for normality to return. Gradually I gained possession of my senses, and the first thing I did was to crawl back to the stream and throw cold water over my head. This served the purpose of clearing

my head at least sufficiently to allow me to think. I took
stock of the situation. What had happened? The answer
was obvious: I had put my horse at a jump and failed to
make it. There was nothing remarkable about that, since
everyone who rides expects to come off occasionally. This
was by no means my first fall, although it was a pretty bad
one. I shuddered a little as I looked at the stream. If I had
landed just a couple of feet farther back, I might have
struck my head on the large stones which lay only inches
below the surface. The result of that could have been fatal,
as I might quite easily have drowned in the shallow water.
I shuddered at the thought of how close I had been to
complete disaster.

After a little while, and feeling a little better, very slowly and somewhat unsteadily I clambered to my feet. I bent
each leg and flexed my fingers. There did not appear to be
anything seriously wrong. I would, of course, be a mass of
bruises, but everything—arms, legs, and so on—seemed to
be in good working order. I looked around for Honey, but
of course there was no sign of him. In the manner of his
kind, he would have returned directly to his stable. It was
then that I spotted my saddle. It was lying in the water a
few inches from the edge. Slowly I walked over to where it
lay and pulled it out of the stream. I found the effort quite
painful, but it told me what I wanted to know. The girth
had snapped off at the leather straps which attach it to the
saddle. Well, I thought as I recovered my breath after that
exertion, it was not bad horsemanship or a bad horse, but
bad equipment. It gave me some satisfaction to realize
that Ormerod would not be able to blame me for this.

I decided to leave the saddle where it was, since there
was no point in trying to take it back to the house. In my
bruised and battered condition, I doubt if I could have
carried it, anyway. I picked up my top hat from where it
lay and looked at it sadly; it had been a nice topper but
now it was all battered and ripped. Thank goodness I was

wearing it, I thought; at least it had served its purpose. I
put it down beside the saddle, picked my way gingerly up
the bank, and painfully started off in the direction of the
house.

I looked forward to my walk with a complete absence
of enthusiasm; it was about a mile from Blawath Beck to
Goathlands, and most of the way was uphill. I felt so miserable; my body was a mass of aches and pains, I could
feel the bruises starting, and I knew from experience that
they would get worse. My beautiful broadcloth habit was
all muddied and covered with green slime, and it clung to
me with a cold and clammy embrace. To top everything, I
was soaking wet from the waist downwards. However, I
realized that I had to get back as soon as possible. The
faster I could get into a hot bath and soak away those
aches and pains, the sooner my bruises would cease to
trouble me.

I looked with distaste at the rising moorland that stood
between me and Goathlands. Goathlands stood far off in
the distance. I plodded on step by step. I wanted to cry,
but I could not spare the energy.

I could not have been going for more than a hundred
yards when away to my right I saw two riders. They were
about a mile from me when I spotted them trotting along
the top of Northdale Scar. I realized straight away that
they must be looking for me. Honey must have been seen
when he got back to the stable yard. Seeing him there
saddleless, Ormerod would have at once arranged for a
search. How wise of him, I thought, always to insist on
knowing where one was going if one took a horse out
alone.

I waved in the direction of the riders; it was only a moment before they saw me. One of them pointed toward
me, and they set off in a brisk canter in my direction. As
they got a little nearer, I recognized Henry and Ormerod.

Henry, riding a big black mare, soon left Ormerod behind on his stocky Irish Cob. As Henry got to me, he leapt from the saddle. Letting the mare go loose to be picked up by Ormerod, he rushed over to where I was standing.

"Emma, are you all right?" he cried, his voice full of concern.

"I think so," I replied. "I had a fall."

"Are you all right, Miss Emma?" Ormerod had caught Henry's mare and ridden up and dismounted.

"Yes, thank you, Ormerod," I replied.

"Ormerod saw Honey come back into the yard," said Henry. "We've been terribly worried. What happened?"

"I was trying a jump and I think the girth broke," I answered. "You'll find the saddle down there by the beck." I indicated the direction from which I had come.

"Don't bother about that now," replied Henry. "The first thing to do is to get you back to the house. Do you think you can manage to sit in front of me, or would you rather walk?"

"I'll try sitting in front," I said. It would not be comfortable, but I certainly did not want to walk if that was at all avoidable.

"Right," said Henry. "I'll mount, then you can put her up, Ormerod."

He got back onto his horse, sitting behind the saddle. Ormerod asked him to wait a moment while he moved the saddle as far forward as he could, and then he lifted me up gently and sat me on the saddle. He adjusted the left stirrup leather so that I could get one foot in and thus give myself a little balance. Henry then put one arm on either side of me and held the reins in front of me.

"Do you think you'll be all right like that?" he asked. I assured him that I would.

"We'll start right away," he said, turning to Ormerod. "You get the saddle and catch us up." We headed off up the hill at a slow walk.

Ormerod went off in the direction of the beck to collect

the saddle. I started to thank Henry for his kindness and concern, but he stopped me, telling me that I was not to talk but to try and relax until we got home. In a few minutes Ormerod rejoined us, with my saddle slung over his horse's withers and my poor topper in his hand.

"I fear thou'll not be using this again, Miss Emma," he said, indicating the hat.

I smiled at him but did not reply. We rode on in silence. It was not too uncomfortable for me. I held on to the mounting lock on the mare's mane while Henry's arms on either side of me gave me added support. Ormerod rode alongside us, grim faced and silent. I knew exactly what was worrying him. Whatever went wrong with the horses, he always regarded it as his own personal responsibility, and here he had been presented with a broken girth. In Ormerod's mind, he and he alone was responsible for my fall, though I did not envy the grooms when he made his inquiry.

At last we arrived at the front of the house. Ormerod helped me down, and then Henry dismounted and handed his mare to him. Ormerod led the animals away.

"Now then, coz," said Henry. "Do you think you can make it upstairs, or would you like me to give you a hand?"

"I'll be able to manage," I said. "Thank you for coming for me, Henry."

"Can't take chances, can we?" he said, smiling. "Now, you go up to your room, and I'll find Dr. Harrison and tell her to come and have a look at you."

I was about to protest that I did not need a doctor, but Henry was already on his way.

Slowly and painfully, for my bruises were beginning to hurt by that time, I made my way upstairs and into my sitting room. When I got there I rang for Letty and stood, dripping, in front of the fire.

"Oh, miss!" said Letty as she came into the room, regarding me with astonishment. "What happened, are you all right?"

"I fell off my horse, Letty, but I'm all right," I reassured her. "Now be a good girl and get me a pot of strong tea and then run me a hot bath while I drink it, meanwhile I'll get out of these wet things."

"Yes, miss." She scuttled into the bedroom, returning a moment later. "I've put your dressing gown out. I'm so sorry, miss." She ran off.

Poor Letty, she really did sound concerned. Well, it was nice to know that she cared.

I limped into my bedroom and stripped off my wet clothes. I was just slipping into my dressing gown when Letty came back.

"Dr. Harrison is here, miss, she says Mr. Henry said she had to see you."

I had no particular desire to see Dr. Harrison, but it was not possible to be rude. After all, she had taken the trouble to come over and see me, so I went back into the sitting room and greeted her.

"How do you feel, Miss Waldron?" she asked, her tone cold and businesslike.

"A bit bruised, but apart from that I feel all right. I told Henry not to bother you."

"I am sure that you will allow me to be the judge of whether or not my presence is necessary," she said. "Were you unconscious at all?"

"I don't recall, I'm not really sure," I answered. "Everything was very hazy for a time, I may have been knocked out, but I couldn't say for certain."

"I see," she said. "If you had been unconscious it is quite likely that you would not recall the fact that it occurred. Tell me all that you can remember about the accident."

"Well, I do remember putting Honey at the jump, and

then I was lying on the bank, and that's about all." It did not seem very much but it really was all that I could recall.

"I understand," she said, taking my pulse as she spoke. "Well, I don't think that there is anything serious, but I should like you to take it easy for at least the rest of today. Have a hot bath and go to bed, and apart from a little stiffness, you'll feel a lot better tomorrow morning."

She left me. It was kind of her to come, but I did find myself wishing that I could see her smile just once.

I had a cup of strong sweet tea and then got into my bath. The water was hot and deep and I soaked myself for a good half hour, topping up the water and keeping it as hot as I could bear it. Eventually, I got out of the bath, dried myself, slipped once again into my dressing gown, and went back to the sitting room. Uncle Joshua was standing there waiting for me.

I could scarcely believe my eyes. I realized that what I was witnessing was an unprecedented event. Uncle Joshua never left his rooms in the west wing, and yet here he was in my sitting room. For the second time within a week, and on both occasions on my account, he had left his quarters. He had not even gone out to watch Kittiwake or to see his guests of the last two days.

"Thank God you are all right, Emma," he said, holding his hand out to me.

"Uncle Josh," I cried, taking his outstretched hand and kissing him on the cheek. "How kind of you to come and see me."

"Dear little Emma," he said. "I heard about Honey coming back alone, and then Henry told me about your fall. I simply had to find out for myself that all was well. And I must apologise for just walking in here, but I did knock and there was no answer."

"I was taking a bath," I explained. "And you're not to worry about me. It's nothing more than a couple of bruises."

"May I sit with you for a little while?" he asked.

"Of course," I replied. "There is nothing that I should like better."

He sat in the armchair by the fire. During the next half an hour or so, he poured his heart out to me. Since the death of my aunt he had been a lonely man, but how lonely I found it hard to imagine. Not that he was alone in the physical sense, there were plenty of people at Goathlands, but he lacked love and affection. What a great pity that he and Henry had never had any warmth in their relationship. I knew, of course, that he had always been fond of me, but until then I had never realized just how deep his feelings toward me were. Uncle Joshua loved me as if I were the daughter that he had always wanted but had never had. He admitted to me that when Henry had suggested to him that I might do the typewriting, he had leapt at the idea, though in truth it was really a ruse to persuade me to come back here.

Gradually our conversation became less intense, and we started talking about the old days when grandpapa was alive. Every other sentence began with, "Do you remember?" When finally he took his leave, I sat there for a long time, gazing at the pictures made by the hot coals in the fire. I realized how important my being here was to him, and more, I realized that if I was the daughter he had never had, then he was equally the father I had lost.

My muscles were beginning to stiffen and the bruises were beginning to hurt, so I left my fire and climbed painfully into bed. As I lay there letting drowsiness creep over me, I thought how nice it was to be back. I thought about Uncle Josh and how nice it was to feel loved and needed. Most certainly, now that I knew how much he wanted me to stay, I should never dream of leaving him now. Then I let my mind wander to Henry. I remembered how it was he who had rushed out to search for me as soon as he suspected that there had been an accident. A strange man, my cousin, and yet there was something very nice about him. I wondered if perhaps he was in some financial difficulty. If this was to prove the case, I might be able to help there. Possibly a word from me to Uncle Josh might unloose the purse strings; I would have to think about that. Even Dr. Harrison had shown concern today; at least I thought she had, albeit hidden under her coldly professional exterior. I wondered whether she ever showed her emotions to anyone, though I didn't doubt that she was devoted to Uncle Joshua. That left Roger. Why, I asked myself, were my feelings always so vulnerable in his presence? I had never ever met a man who could irritate me so easily. A remark which I would have ignored if made by anyone else would raise my hackles and put me on the defensive right away if it came from Roger. Oh, bother Roger, I thought. I put him out of my mind.

I decided that I really could not complain about my fall. It had been a pure accident, and it had certainly shown me the nicer side of Henry and the love of Uncle Joshua. No, I said to myself, I could not complain. In some strange way, I was glad that I had had my accident.

I was soon asleep. The whole day had been quite exhausting, and it seemed no time at all before I heard the swish of the curtains as Letty opened them the following morning.

"Please, miss, Mr. Ormerod says could you go over to the stables after breakfast," she said, putting the tea tray onto my bed.

"Did he say what it was about?" I was a little surprised; it was an unusual request.

"No, miss, but it seemed to be important. I thought he seemed a bit excited, which is not like Mr. Ormerod."

It was certainly not at all like Ormerod to be excited; he was always so cool and calm whatever happened.

"Tell him I shall see him as soon as I can get away," I said. "And Letty, will you take my riding habit and see what you can do about it? It's rather a mess, I'm afraid."

"I washed it last night when you was asleep, miss," she replied. "It's all right, it isn't torn. I'll iron it today and bring it up."

"Thank you, Letty, you are most thoughtful," I said as she left me.

I wondered what it was that Ormerod wanted to see me about. I did hope that there was nothing wrong with Honey; anyhow, whatever it was, it would have to keep until I saw him.

I got out of bed rather gingerly. I felt very stiff and I had a nasty bruise on my hip, but all in all it was not too bad. It was certainly not as bad as I had expected. Dressing proved a little painful, but I managed. I went down to breakfast at about a quarter to nine. I was quite surprised to find that Roger was still there.

"Hello there," he said. "Come and sit down while I get you some breakfast. We must look after the wounded, or what would Miss Nightingale say? What would you like?"

"Are there any kidneys?" I asked.

"Sorry ma'am, I just ate the last of them." When I pouted he said, "Of course it was done deliberately and because I knew that you would want them."

I had to laugh. "Kippers?" I asked hesitantly.

"Kippers do not seem too popular today, madam, there are three left. Will you eat them all?"

"Good Heavens, no," I said. "One will be plenty." Roger's cheerful banter was just the thing to chase away the remaining aches and pains.

"One kipper." He placed it before me. "Tea or coffee?"

"Coffee, please."

We chatted away while I ate my breakfast, and again I found myself warming to this man. I found that I was enjoying his company more than I cared to admit.

Breakfast over, it was time to go and see Ormerod.

Roger accompanied me as far as the big barn. I left him there with Kittiwake and carried on to the stables.

When I arrived there, I found Ormerod waiting for me. He was standing, grim faced, talking to one of the grooms. As soon as he saw me, he left his companion and came toward me.

"You wanted to see me, I believe?" I said.

"That's right, Miss Emma," he replied. "I think thou'd better come into the tack room with me."

He strode purposefully toward the tack room, and I followed. I wondered what on earth could be the matter. Ormerod was abrupt, almost brusque in his manner. It was not like him; I don't think that I had ever seen him in this sort of mood. We went into the tack room with its lovely smell of polished leather and its shining brasses. All the harnesses were neatly arranged and hanging from hooks bearing the names of the horses. The other groom was there when we arrived; he was sitting on a stool saddle soaping some harness.

"Out," Ormerod said to him. "You can finish that when Miss Emma leaves."

"Now then," I said. "You had better tell me what all of this is about." I was beginning to feel somewhat uneasy about the whole business.

"Miss Emma, when I found out, I wasn't sure that I should tell thee." His tone was serious. "I would not want to be the one to worry thee, of all people. It is for thy own safety that I must tell thee what I found."

"Then tell me what this thing is that you found." I was becoming quite alarmed. "There's something wrong with Honey, I'm not going to be able to ride him again?"

"Nay, lass, there's nothing wrong with the horse. I only wish that that was what it is. Here, you'd better take a look at this."

He went over to a corner and pulled away a blanket revealing my saddle. I noticed, to my surprise, that it had not been cleaned and that the girth was still attached. I went over to examine it.

"Well?" I asked.

"Look at the straps on the girth, Miss Emma."

I looked. The straps were still attached to the buckles of the girth, but the stitching which had attached them to the saddle had torn away.

"I see," I said, for it was indeed what I had expected to see, either that or torn leather. "The stitching ripped and that is why the girth broke."

"Nay, Miss Emma," replied Ormerod. "That stitching never ripped, it were cut."

Chapter Ten

FOR A MOMENT I stood speechless. The beautiful world which I had created in my imagination had, in one shattering moment, crashed around me. I thought of all those lovely people who had been so kind to me. One of them must have done this terrible thing. Dearly though I would have loved to have found some other possible explanation, there could be none. It had to be one of them. I knew now that someone here hated me, hated me enough to want to harm me physically or even kill me. I looked down at the broken girth and then at Ormerod's grim face. I clutched at one last straw of hope; could Ormerod possibly be mistaken?

"Ormerod," I said in a quiet voice. "Are you quite certain that this was deliberate?"

"It couldn't be no other way, Miss Emma. Do thou

think I should have worried thee if there could have been another possibility?" His voice was grave. "Look thee here." He held up the end of the girth, showing me the straps. "See how the stitching is all torn and ragged for the top half inch? That were where it ripped when thou took the jump. Now look at the rest of the straps, clean cut through for more than five inches. When stitching goes, it don't break at each hole, it snaps here and there and the thread pulls through, leaving it all ragged. Look at these straps, the thread is still in all of the holes. It was deliberate all right, somebody slid a knife between the strap and the saddle and just left that top half-inch attached. What we've got to do now is to find out who."

What he said was true; I knew it as soon as I asked him the question. Ormerod would never have alarmed me if he had not been certain.

It all came flooding back to me; the missing teddy bear, the burnt papers. Nana was no accident, and the burning of the papers had nothing to do with Kittiwake, but with me. And now this. What would happen next? I asked myself. I only knew that the answer would not be pleasant.

"But who would want to do such a thing?" I cried.

"And to thee of all people, Miss Emma." Ormerod was very cool and very angry. I had never seen him like this before. "Whoever he is, when I lay my hands on him, I'll kill him." He held his hands up and looked at them. "I'll kill him with these two hands."

It was quite terrifying to watch him. "Ormerod, I want you to promise me something," I said. "I want you to promise me that you will not do anything foolish."

" 'Twould be naught but justice, Miss Emma. How I would like to get my hands around his throat."

I shuddered. "Promise me," I insisted. My concern was not only for the possible victim but also for Ormerod. I would have loathed to see Ormerod get into trouble on my account.

"All right, Miss Emma, it shall be as you say. I promise," he said grudgingly.

"Ormerod," I continued, "who knows about this?"

"Just thee and me and the one as did it."

"Then I need another promise from you. I want you to promise me that you will not breathe a word about this to anyone."

The thought had entered my mind that, should this news get to Uncle Joshua's ears, he might take it very badly. Above all, I did not want to have him worried.

"But why, Miss Emma? We ought to tell the police at least."

"Ormerod, you must trust me. I have my reasons," I said. "They are very good reasons."

"Just as thou wish, miss, I can't say as how I approve," he replied.

I realized that I either had to change the subject or tell him everything, and I was not ready to tell him yet.

"What are you going to do about the saddle?" I asked.

"I'll repair it myself, Miss Emma. I'll take it down to my cottage tonight, that way no one will know. Miss Emma, if thou want to go riding again, tell me, I'll see to thy tack personal." He paused. "Hardly seems credible that anyone could have done such a thing, do it?"

"I don't understand either, Ormerod," I said. "I did not believe that I had an enemy in the world."

I finally left Ormerod and made my way slowly back to the house. The sky was beginning to cloud over. As I looked up at the walls of the house, I thought how warm and secure they had appeared yesterday and how grim and full of menace they seemed now. I did not go through the big barn, because Roger would be in there, and I had no desire to talk to anyone at all. I felt so desperately alone and uncertain of everything that I wanted to scream. Who could I approach for comfort and counsel? There was only

Uncle Joshua, and it would be out of the question to speak to him about my worries.

My slow reluctant steps finally brought me to the front door, and I went in. Barton was standing in the hall.

"Miss Emma, I have been looking for you. Cook would like to have a word with you when you have a moment to spare," he said.

"Not today, Barton," I replied. "Tell her that I will see her tomorrow, and that if it is something which can't wait, I am sure that her judgment will be every bit as good as mine."

I could not bear the thought of dealing with everyday household matters. I felt I simply had to be alone. I escaped from Barton and went up to my room, flopped down in the armchair by the fire, and wept.

Lunch time came and went and I did not go down. Though I knew that I would have to face them soon enough, I could not bear the thought of sitting down at table with them just then. I think that that was the most frightening thing about all of this; it had become "them" and me. Any one of them could be my tormentor, and until I found out who, there was no one whom I dared trust.

Promptly at four o'clock, Letty brought in my afternoon tea. I noticed, to my dismay, that there were two cups on the tray.

"Why two cups?" I asked her.

"For Mr. Henry, miss. He said that he was going to join you for tea."

"Oh, no," I said. "Letty, please tell him that I can't see him." I was being cowardly I knew, for I would have to face them all soon, and putting it off was not going to make it any easier.

"Oh, miss." Letty was dismayed. "I couldn't say a thing like that to Mr. Henry."

It seemed that I was not the only coward present. The problem was solved, however, by Henry, who appeared in the open door at that moment.

"What is it you couldn't say to Mr. Henry?" he asked.

"Henry, I do hope you will understand, but I told Letty that I did not feel like entertaining anyone," I answered him.

"I'm sorry to hear that," he replied. "Are you still feeling a bit under the weather, coz?"

Was it my imagination, or was Henry avoiding looking me in the eye as he spoke?

"Well, I think it's a shame." He had taken my silence as an affirmation. "Don't worry, if you would rather I didn't stay, I'll go, and I promise not to be offended." He spoke kindly enough. "Shall we see you at dinner?"

"Yes, I'll be down to dinner," I replied. "I'll be all right by then."

There, I had committed myself. It was better that I had, for I could not continue putting off and putting off.

"Come now, Letty, out we go, let's leave Miss Emma alone," said Henry.

With a nod, he left me, and Letty scuttled out. Once again I was alone with my thoughts.

All too soon it was half past six, and the sound of the dressing gong reverberated through the house. Letty appeared and asked me what I intended wearing for dinner. At first I was inclined to wear anything which came to hand, but I decided against this. I was sure that if I dressed well I should feel better and perhaps manage to get rid of some of the depression which was overshadowing me. I possessed a beautiful ball gown of pale green silk chiffon, and that was what I chose to wear. Letty was most surprised; she assured me that it was just an ordinary dinner. Little did she know how extraordinary it in fact was.

At seven-thirty the gong sounded for dinner. I looked at

myself in the mirror. Under almost any other circumstances I should have found the result most pleasing. As it was, I tried to smile at my reflection but found it very difficult. I waited three or four minutes before going down to the dining room. I did not want to find myself alone with any single person, so I waited to give them time to assemble. It was about five and twenty minutes to eight when I made my move and went down.

Henry, Roger, and Dr. Harrison were already seated at the table when I entered. Henry and Roger rose to greet me.

"Good evening," I said, taking my place at the head of the table. "Please sit down."

"May I be permitted to say how lovely you look?" said Roger.

"Hear, hear," said Henry.

Dr. Harrison concurred with a slight raising of her eyebrows and a little nod.

I looked at each of them in turn. How strange fate had been to thrust the four of us together. If you had searched the length and breadth of the land, I doubt if you could have found a quartet who had so little in common. Roger and Dr. Harrison were both dedicated people, but dedicated to ideas so far apart; there could be no common ground between engineering and medicine. Then there was Henry, likeable, irresponsible, and thoroughly spoilt, not really caring about anything. And me? What was I? A victim to one of them or just a fool who ought to get out of this place?

Barton served the soup and I sat looking from one to the other as they drank theirs. Dr. Harrison sat bolt upright, taking prim little sips from a half-filled spoon. Henry was, as always, fastidious, correct, and perfectly mannered, waiting until I had dipped my spoon into my soup before he started and dabbing the corner of his mouth with his napkin about every third mouthful. Roger ate in the same manner that he seemed to do everything else, with boisterous enthusiasm, finishing well ahead of the rest of us.

It occurred to me that I was being somewhat ridiculous. Surely they would notice how I was so intently watching each of them in turn. I had no idea what it was that I expected to find out. It was highly improbable that my enemy would reveal him or herself by the manner in which he handled a soup spoon.

"When are you planning to take your horse out again?" Roger was talking to me.

I stiffened and dropped my spoon. Dr. Harrison immediately retrieved it for me.

"Are you still not feeling well?" she asked.

"Thank you, I am perfectly well," I replied.

"Are you quite sure, coz?" said Henry.

"Of course I'm sure," I replied, realizing how insincere my answer must sound and watching them to see if I could detect satisfaction in any of their expressions. There was only concern.

"I'm sorry, Roger," I continued. "You asked me something."

Of course I knew perfectly well what he had asked, but what was his motive? Why should he be interested in when I was going to ride again? Was it him? Was there more devilment planned for my next ride?

"I asked you when you intended riding again," he said with a sympathetic smile. "I'm sorry, I don't want to worry you, but after a nasty fall such as you had, it would be a good idea to get on a horse again as soon as possible. You don't want to lose your nerve, do you?"

"He's quite right, you know," said Henry. "You mustn't leave it too long."

"I think I would agree with that," added Dr. Harrison. "But I don't think you should go too soon either."

Each remark had been completely in character, even to

the accompanying facial expression and tone of voice. It told me nothing.

"I have not yet decided," I replied. "But please don't worry about my nerve; it is by no means the first time I have fallen."

I certainly had no intention of revealing any plans I might have had, but as it happened I had given the matter no thought, and so my reply was quite truthful.

By this time, Barton had cleared away the soup things and was serving the main course. As he brought a tray of sizzling lamb chops for my inspection and approval, he murmured, "Will you be able to see cook tomorrow?"

I nodded; life must go on, and for Uncle Joshua's sake I could not neglect all of my duties. The conversation had lapsed while Barton served the meal, apart from Henry's requesting a half-bottle of claret for himself and Roger, Dr. Harrison and I having indicated that we would not be taking wine.

After cutting off a corner of my lamb chop and spearing it with my fork, so that the others could start, I put my knife and fork down and gazed at my meal with a rising feeling of nausea. It was impossible for me to get it out of my mind that I was sitting there in the presence of my tormentor. But who? Who and why? That question kept pounding into my head. If I could only answer the first part of it: who? If I could only stand up there and then and point my finger and say, "You are the one. You are the one who cut my girth, it was you who burnt my papers. Now you must tell me why." After all, what had I ever done to any of them? What cause was there for anyone here to hate me? In what manner or means could I possibly present a threat? But then, supposing none of this was true, supposing it was an illogical hatred, a threat based on the fantasy of a sick mind? Supposing that this was the truth? Then it was more than just an enemy I had to deal with; it was madness.

I was watching them again; they were eating their meal as if not one of them had a care in the world. How dare they, I thought, while I was sitting there almost sick with fear and apprehension. I had to try and pull myself together. These were foolish thoughts which could not help me in any conceivable way. They were dangerous too. I realized that if I did not control myself they could take possession of me and make me hysterical. Even worse, perhaps I would drive myself mad.

I picked up my fork, still containing the piece of lamb chop I had cut earlier. It was getting cold, and the fat was beginning to congeal. I put it down again with a feeling of disgust.

Roger said, "Come on, Emma, eat your dinner. It's not poisoned, you know."

I let out a gasp of horror. Poison. Dear God, not that.

"I say, did I say something to upset you? I'm awfully sorry," said Roger.

"No, I replied. "Please forgive me, I . . . I don't think I am very hungry."

"Now look here, Miss Waldron," said Dr. Harrison. "You must eat something. Henry, would you ring for Barton?"

I started to protest.

"No, Miss Waldron," continued Dr. Harrison. "Tell Barton what you want, but I am going to insist that you eat. You assured us that it was just a fall and that you are perfectly all right. Now I am speaking as a doctor, and I want you to be sensible and have a little to eat and then go up to your room and go to bed."

"She's quite right, you know," said Henry as Barton came in. "You've got to have something."

I gave in and asked Barton to bring me an omelette. He was worried that I had not enjoyed my dinner, but I assured him that it was me and not the meal.

They all sat and watched me while I ate, two of them I

was sure with genuine concern, but which two? After I had eaten, I left them and went upstairs. There was no point in arguing with Dr. Harrison's logic even had I disagreed with her, and I knew that she was right. I got to my room, locked myself in, and went to bed. I was not going to take any more chances. Tomorrow I would seriously consider my situation here.

It was with this thought that I fell asleep.

Chapter Eleven

I WAS AWAKENED by a loud knocking. I got out of bed, slipped into my dressing gown, and went to the locked sitting room door.

"Who's there?" I demanded nervously.

"It's me, miss, Letty," replied a voice. "I've brought your tea, miss."

Good gracious, I thought, it must be eight o'clock. I unlocked the door and let Letty in. I was surprised at how well I must have slept. Whatever else my troubles had done to me, they had not interfered with that.

"Are you sure that you're all right, miss?" asked Letty, putting my tray down.

Poor girl, she must have had a surprise at finding her entrance barred.

"Yes, Letty," I replied. "There is nothing wrong. I have just decided to sleep with my door locked; don't let it worry you."

"It doesn't worry me, miss. I always sleep with my door locked, but I won't be able to get in in the morning."

"You'll just have to knock as you did this morning,

Letty," I answered. "You can leave the tray there and get my gray tweed out. I shall be going out this morning after I have seen cook, and I may not be back until after lunch."

I had decided to take the pony and trap and go down to Goathland Village. It was my intention to call on the vicar. I had no special plan in mind, but I wanted desperately to get away from the house for a few hours and give myself time to think. I did not know whether I would say anything to the Reverend Cox about my experiences. In any case, it would be nice to talk to him. He had been vicar of Goathland for as long as I could remember, a big kindly man with a heart as large as his frame. He was regarded by the local tramps as the easiest touch in Yorkshire.

By the time I had finished my tea, Letty had made my bed and neatly laid out my clothes.

"Shall I help you dress, miss?" she asked.

"No thank you, Letty," I replied. "You can take the tray and go now."

Letty left me. I dressed slowly, and it was after nine when I finally made my way out of my rooms. As soon as I stepped out into the corridor, I felt vulnerable. Inside my own quarters I felt a certain amount of security. I could lock the door, shut the world out, and feel safe from the threat which hung over me. Once outside of those walls, I became a target for my unknown tormentor and a prey to my own imagination.

I walked slowly to the dining room, pausing at every corner to insure that no one was in sight. I saw not a soul until I got to the dining room, where, to my dismay, I found that Roger was still there. I had resolved that I would, from now on, try to avoid any situation which would leave me alone with only one other person, but what could I do now? I got the distinct impression that he had been waiting for me.

Could he be the one? Could this handsome, courageous man have another side to his character? A dark and sinister side? I looked at him; it was hardly credible, but then was it any more credible that it should be either of the others? I stopped involuntarily as I caught sight of him.

"Hello there," he said, brushing his unruly forelock back into place. "I've saved you some kidneys. Sit down and I'll get them for you."

Kidneys. Yes, they all knew that I liked kidneys for breakfast, and was it not Roger who had said something about poison at dinner last night? I made a quick decision.

"I think I'd rather have sausages if there are any," I replied.

"You're in luck, there are some left," he said. "And I think I'll join you, if you don't mind."

I did not reply, and I suppose he took my silence as assent. He attended to my needs, just as he had done the previous morning, chattering away all the while. For myself, I hardly spoke at all. He told me that he was going to fly Kittiwake again that day and asked me if I would like to watch. I told him that I had to go down to the village and doubted whether I should be back in time.

"By the way," he said. "I hope you didn't mind my waiting for you, but Sir Joshua was wondering if perhaps you were still not feeling too well. I promised to find out. You didn't go and see him at all yesterday, did you?"

Poor Uncle Josh. In spite of what had happened, it was cruel of me to forget him.

"No, I didn't," I replied. "That was wrong of me. I'll go and see him as soon as I finish breakfast."

"Well, it so happens that I have an appointment with him at a quarter to ten. I'll tell him what you said, and you could go and see him when you return from the village. I can't delay my appointment if we are going to get Kittiwake into the air today."

"All right, I'll do that," I replied. "Tell him I would like to come and take tea with him this afternoon, and tell him I am sorry that I didn't come yesterday."

"I'm sure that will please him," said Roger. "Well, it's almost a quarter to. I'd better be off, mustn't keep the old boy waiting."

I finished breakfast, and as I was leaving the dining room I caught sight of Henry crossing the hall. I stepped back into the room and stood there until he had gone. I did not want to explain my intended movements to anyone. I realized that I had already told Roger where I was going and that that was a mistake. The fewer people who knew in advance where I would be, the better. I went down to the kitchen, as I had promised, and settled a few domestic problems with cook. Then I left the house by the tradesmen's entrance and headed toward the stables.

When I got there, I found Ormerod in the tack room and asked him to prepare a pony and trap for me. He told me that it would take about twenty minutes, and when I said I would wait for it, he produced the inevitable apple and told me to go and talk to Honey while he got it ready. He made no mention of the cut girth, apart from telling me that my saddle had been repaired, but I noticed that he did not delegate the responsibility for preparing the pony and trap to either of the grooms.

I returned to the stable yard some fifteen minutes later and found Ormerod, having already gotten the pony between the shafts, inspecting every stitch and buckle on the harness. Finally he seemed satisified and handed the trap over to me. There was a gray pony in the shafts that I had not seen before. Ormerod introduced us; her name was Hazel. I got into the trap and set off down the drive across Howl Moor toward Wheeldale Beck and Goathland Village.

It was a pleasant day, but there was a slight nip in the air from the light easterly breeze which was blowing in from the North Sea some eight miles away. Hazel proved a good carriage pony, staying in an extended trot for the whole journey, picking her feet up well and giving me a very pleasant ride.

One's relationship with animals is a strange thing. Had Honey been between the shafts, I should have poured out my troubles to him all the way to the village. Hazel and I had, however, only just been introduced, and one does not impart confidences to a comparative stranger. So I sat silently in the trap, brooding over the events which had occurred in what was really an incredibly short period, since my return to Goathlands.

We arrived at the church and I drove up the drive, round behind the graveyard and up to the front door of the vicarage. This was a typical example of the kind of house that the Church of England provides for its pastors. Much too large, much too cold, much too rambling, and much too expensive to maintain on the stipend of a country parson. Mr. Cox answered the door himself and greeted me warmly. He did not seem surprised to see me, but Mr. Cox never seemed surprised at anything. He led me into his sparsely furnished sitting room; there was no fire and it was quite chilly. Mrs. Cox appeared and suggested that we go into the kitchen, it being the warmest room in the house. We would still be able to talk privately there, as it was their cook-general's day off.

We sat and chatted and drank tea for about an hour. The conversation was general, pleasant and inconsequential. I felt very warmly toward Mr. Cox and I think I would have told him about my frightening experiences over the last few days, but I found the extra presence even of Mrs. Cox somewhat inhibiting. By the time I felt I had to leave, I had talked a lot and said nothing. They came to the front door and said goodbye to me with promises to call soon.

I was feeling better, free of the cloud which hung over me at Goathlands. I drove round to the front of the church, stopped, and went inside. There is something strangely comforting about the atmosphere of an empty church, especially if it is very old, and this one had stood there for about six centuries. It is as if all the prayers which had ever been said there were still around, giving the feeling of goodness, warmth, and calm. I sat in one of the rear pews, the one which, every Sunday, was reserved for the staff from Goathlands. I remember noticing that it was, in fact, Ormerod's place in which I was sitting.

My prayer was not specific; in fact, I do not remember praying consciously at all. I felt that it was not necessary, for God knew what my troubles were, Even though I had not formulated it in words, He would, in His own way, answer my plea for help.

I do not know how long I stayed there, but when, with some reluctance, I left, I felt hungry. I decided that I would lunch at the inn at Mallyan Spout. I suppose that it was not very ladylike to go there unescorted, but the landlord and his wife were both friends of the family so I was sure that it would be all right.

The inn, an old Tudor coaching house, stood about half a mile out of Goathland Village. When I arrived, I received a most warm welcome from the landlord, who insisted that I take lunch with his wife and himself. The time passed quickly over a lovely meal of mutton pie and talk of the old days. Before I realized it, it was three o'clock.

Remembering that I had promised to take tea with Uncle Josh, I made my apologies to my host and hostess. When we emerged from the inn, it was not a very heartening sight which met our eyes. Less than a hundred yards away, a great bank of cloud which reached right down to the ground was slowly rolling toward us.

In that part of Yorkshire, the fog will sometimes roll in from the sea and cover the whole countryside in an impenetrable blanket of damp gray mist. I knew at once that that was what must have been happening. As Goathlands

stood between Mallyan Spout and the sea, the chances
were that the whole journey home would be in fog. My
hosts suggested that I stay at the inn, and they would send
a rider to tell the people at Goathlands that I should not
be returning that day. I thanked them for their kind offer,
but felt I had to refuse. I could not bear the thought of letting Uncle Josh down again. There was not, I considered,
any real danger from the fog, apart from its being unpleasant. I would have much more chance of getting back to
Goathlands than their rider would have of finding it.
Hazel, given her head, would, like any other horse, go
straight back to her stable. So, feeling quite confident even
if I did not relish the trip, I climbed into the trap and we
started on our way.

Within a minute we were cocooned in the fog. It was as
thick as I can ever remember seeing it. Hazel slowed to a
walk and I tied the reins to the bar on the front board of
the trap. I attached them loosely so as to leave her head
free. She stopped while I was doing this, like the well-
schooled animal she was. I tapped her lightly with the
whip, and she started off at a trot which soon slowed to a
walk when she discovered that she was able to choose her
own pace.

The fog was so thick that I could barely see Hazel's
ears. The stillness and silence were so intense that they
seemed to have body and form. Hazel stooped quite frequently to crop a mouthful of grass, but whenever I saw
her head go down I tapped her with the whip and she
moved on.

I found myself straining to catch any sound other than
the faint creaking of the harness, Hazel's breathing, and
the slow, steady clop, clop, clop, as her feet hit the ground.

I do not think that I am naturally claustrophobic, but
the tiny gray universe in which I found myself enclosed
was not the sort of world I would have chosen at any time.
Add to that the fact that my nerves were on edge as a re-

sult of the recent events at Goathlands, and I suppose that
it was natural that I should find tension building up within
me. I found myself holding my breath so that I could better use the one sense which was functioning normally in
those conditions, and I listened intently for any signal that
might indicate danger.

Suddenly, I cried aloud in panic and just as quickly realized what had happened. There was a noisy flurry just
ahead of Hazel and then . . . "Pee-whit, pee-whit, pee-
whit." She had disturbed a couple of plovers sheltering in
the grass nearby. They were soon silent again. I supposed
they had alighted somewhere close at hand as soon as they
knew that they were in no danger. This incident made me
aware of the state of my nerves, for it was not the sort of
thing to which, under normal circumstances, I would have
given a second thought.

There was a long, shrill, mournful howl. I caught my
breath and gripped the handrail so tightly that my hands
hurt. I was near to panic; for a moment I imagined that
the devil himself was out on the moor searching for me. I
really had to pull myself together; foxes were not uncom-
mon on Howl Moor and this was the second time within a
week that I had heard the cry of a vixen.

It began to get brighter, and in a moment we were out
of the fog and in blazing sunlight. Two hundred yards
away stood Goathlands, bathed in the afternoon glow. I
looked back at the fog; it was as if the house was standing
on an island in the midst of an ocean of white billowing
cotton wool. A blackbird was singing, and it was all so
beautiful. I untied the reins and trotted Hazel back to the
stable yard.

When we arrived I found Ormerod waiting for us.

"We were getting a bit worried, Miss Emma," he said,
"what with the fog and all."

"We were perfectly safe, Ormerod," I replied. "Has
anyone been asking for me?"

"Mr. Henry was down earlier, he asked if I knew where thou was, and Dr. Harrison came over a little while ago to ask me to tell thee that Sir Joshua would be expecting thee around four o'clock," he answered.

"What time is it now?" I asked.

"Just gone four."

"In that case, I had better go straight in," I said.

Four o'clock indeed, it had taken an hour to cover the two miles from Mallyan Spout.

As I made my way back to the house, I wondered what Henry had wanted. He might have been making what amounted to no more than a casual inquiry, or perhaps he had wanted to arrange a meeting, as his last attempts had both been frustrated. Perhaps he . . . ? But no; I must stop jumping to conclusions. I had to observe and wait, hoping that my enemy would make some sort of error and thus reveal his or her identity.

Uncle Joshua, wearing his skullcap and patch, greeted me warmly when I arrived at his rooms. Tea had already been served and I noticed that there was only one cup on the tray.

"Shall I ring for another cup?" I asked.

"Emma, my dear," he replied. "I am conscious of the fact that the sight of my taking food is not a very pretty one. I shall feel much more comfortable if you will forgive me and just serve yourself."

Poor Uncle Josh, so aware of his deformities and so considerate of my feelings. I tried to explain to him that I did not mind, but he would have none of it. I served myself and nibbled at a couple of the inevitable pink cakes while we talked.

We discussed a variety of subjects, including the books of Monsieur Jules Verne. My uncle was very enthusiastic about these books. He maintained that M. Verne was a prophet; had not the advent of flying machines proved this?

"But this is surely the least of his prophecies," I complained. "There are many other ideas in his works which are completely fantastic."

Uncle Josh insisted that these ideas were not so far-fetched as one might assume. He even suggested that, before the end of this century, men would fly to the moon. Of course I regarded that suggestion as utterly fantastic, but Uncle Josh insisted that it was more than a mere possibility.

An hour soon passed, and I was quite overwhelmed by the simple joy which my companionship seemed to give to this dear man. He seemed so happy in my company that I promised that I would come and spend an hour with him every day.

At last he suggested that I had had enough of an invalid's company and that it was time to leave. I protested that I was enjoying being with him, but he said if I intended to spend an hour every day with him, then he would ration himself to that. He did not want to bore me.

As I made my way to my rooms, I thought how kind and gentle he was. That hour with him had done so much for my faith in people. It was not a bad world which could produce men like Uncle Josh.

When I got to my sitting room I found, to my surprise, a single rose with a note attached, lying on the occasional table by the armchair. It read:

Sorry you were out, maybe we can have tea tomorrow,
Henry.

How nice, I thought, picking up the flower and heading for the bedroom to put it in water.

I opened the bedroom door and was transfixed by the sight which met my eyes. I clutched my hands to my head and screamed aloud.

Chapter Twelve

EMMA

There on the counterpane over my bed, spelled out in large neat letters, was my name. The letters had been formed by using many small pieces of yellow furry material. That was not all, however, for underneath my name was a further piece of yellow fabric on which were the two button eyes and black embroidered nose and mouth of my teddy bear.

I tore out of the bedroom and slammed the door shut behind me. I leaned my back against it for a moment and tried to take hold of myself, but it was no good; panic began to take control of my senses. I felt like a hunted animal searching for a means of escape. I thought I heard a footstep in the corridor outside. I rushed from the sitting room and ran straight into Letty.

"Why, Miss Emma, what's happened? What's the matter, miss?" she cried.

I half screamed at the poor girl, "Get away from me! Leave me alone! Leave me alone!"

"But, miss, you're bleeding."

"Bleeding?" I opened my hand, letting Henry's rose fall to the ground. She was right, there was blood on my hand.

"It's not your hand, it's your head, miss. Let me take you to Dr. Harrison, Miss Emma, she'll soon put you right."

By this time I was in a sort of daze and only partially aware of what was happening. I did know, however, that I did not want to see Dr. Harrison, but I found myself quite incapable of resistance, either physical or verbal, when Letty took me by the arm and gently but firmly led me toward the doctor's rooms. I remember the thought crossing my mind that, in spite of her slight build, Letty was quite strong.

When we arrived at the doctor's rooms we found, to my relief, that they were empty. My relief was momentary, for Letty, nothing deterred, took me inside and sat me down.

"Letty," I said weakly. "I don't want to see Dr. Harrison. I don't want to see anybody. Please, Letty, let me go."

"Don't you worry, miss, the doctor won't be long," she said, ignoring my request. "Here, miss." She offered me a handkerchief. "You could hold this against your head until she comes. It's quite clean, miss, it's just been washed and I haven't used it."

"Thank you, Letty," I said, taking the handkerchief and dabbing it against the cut on my right temple. "You're a good friend, Letty."

"You're very good to me, miss," she replied. "This is my first chance to be a lady's maid. I know I'm not very bright and I've made a lot of mistakes, but you've been very kind."

"I will try to be, Letty," I said. "I think I could have been a lot kinder." Then suddenly I said, "Letty, I don't want to see Dr. Harrison."

"And why not, may I inquire?" Dr. Harrison had silently entered the room. She approached me and loomed over me. "Do you doubt my ability to deal with a scratch?"

"Don't touch me! Leave me alone! I don't want any of you near me!"

As I screamed, she slapped me hard across the face. It was certainly effective, for I stopped screaming and started to sob quietly.

"You didn't ought to have hit Miss Emma, doctor," said Letty.

"You be silent, girl," said Dr. Harrison. "I think you had better leave."

"No!" I said firmly, feeling my control returning. "Letty stays with me."

"Just as you wish, Miss Waldron," said the doctor. "I struck you because I have no intention of allowing you to have hysterics here. Now, whether you like it or not, I am going to have a look at your wound."

"Go on, miss, let her look," said Letty. "She is a doctor."

"Thank you for your support, Letty," said Dr. Harrison, without any hint of sarcasm.

I sat tight-lipped and trembling as she washed my temple.

"Do you know what it was that caused this?" she asked.

"I think it was a rose thorn," I replied.

"Well, it is nothing to worry about," she went on. "It is little more than a scratch. I shall just put a dab of iodine on it and a small dressing which you can remove in about an hour after the bleeding has stopped."

She did this and then stepped back to inspect her handiwork.

"Good heavens, Miss Waldron, why are you trembling so?" she asked. "I told you it is nothing, only a scratch."

I felt like a limp rag. I was completely drained, drained of every emotion, every feeling, drained of everything.

"It's not the cut, it's Nana," I whispered.

"Nana?"

"It's her teddy bear, doctor," explained Letty. "She lost it, she told me about it."

"A teddy bear?" Doctor Harrison's voice was grim. "Miss Waldron, am I to understand that you, a grown woman, have been driven to near hysteria over the loss of a teddy bear?"

"Nana is not lost," I whispered.

"Not lost? Perhaps you will be good enough to explain what this all means?"

"You had better come with me to my rooms and I'll show you," I said.

Dr. Harrison looked as if she was about to protest, but then she apparently changed her mind. When she did speak, it was in the soothing tone that one might use with a child.

"Very well, Miss Waldron, you and I shall go and see this teddy bear."

"Shall I go now, miss?" asked Letty.

"No." I was terrified at the thought of being left alone with Dr. Harrison. "Please stay with me, Letty."

I saw Letty glance questioningly toward Dr. Harrison and receive a nod in reply. We then trooped out and across the hall in the direction of my apartments. When we arrived in my sitting room, I stopped; I did not want to go into the bedroom.

"Well?" said Dr. Harrison.

"In the bedroom," I replied, "on the bed."

Dr. Harrison opened the bedroom and stood there framed in the doorway.

"Well?" she said again.

"Don't you see?" I asked.

"I see nothing unusual," she replied.

"Nothing unusual?" I almost screamed.

I pushed past her and into the bedroom. I let out a gasp of horror and seized a bedpost for support.

There, propped up on the pillows in one piece, just as I had known it in childhood, was Nana.

Chapter Thirteen

IN THAT MOMENT I really did begin to doubt my sanity. I gazed horror-struck at the thing on my bed. There could be no doubt about it, it was my teddy bear, and yet, just a little while ago I had seen it in ribbons, spelling out my name on my bed. Or had I?

"Well?" said Dr. Harrison for the third time.

"I . . . it was nothing. . . . I think I must have imagined it," I replied.

"And just what was it that you think that you imagined?" she asked in a slow, deliberate tone.

For a moment I was tempted to tell her everything, but I stopped myself. How could I be sure that she was not the one? A teddy bear which had been miraculously reassembled from a hundred pieces of rag? It was so ridiculous, how could I expect anyone to believe me? Besides, I was beginning to wonder what it was I had seen.

"Miss Waldron," she continued. "It is only two days since you had a nasty fall, and I cannot be certain that you were not concussed, though at first I thought that this was not so. If you think that you are imagining things, be assured that there is nothing to worry about. Concussion can do strange things to people's minds. Are you imagining anything?"

"Are you trying to tell me that you think I am going mad?" I asked without expression.

"That is a foolish thing to say. Of course I don't think that you are going mad," she replied. "I do think that you might not yet have regained complete control. I am quite sure that you will be perfectly well in a couple of days and laugh about all of this, but for now you must try and rest. Are you sleeping well?"

"Perfectly well," I replied.

"That is good. I want to be informed if you have any severe headaches, and I want you to get as much rest and sleep as you can for the next forty-eight hours. I shall ask Barton to send your meals up here and I shall prepare a draught which I want you to take before retiring."

"What are you going to give me?" I asked suspiciously.

"Just a mild sleeping draught of chloral hydrate, it will help you to relax. Come now, Letty, I think it would be well to leave Miss Waldron now and let her rest."

I thanked her for her advice, and she left me, taking Letty with her.

Alone, I went over to the bed and picked up the teddy bear. Suddenly it had become quite repulsive to me, but I examined it closely. There could be no doubt, it was definitely Nana. I opened the door of the wardrobe and flung the offending toy into a far corner. I had no desire to see it again.

I returned to the sitting room and sat by the fire. Why, I asked myself, had I not told Dr. Harrison the whole story? I was beginning to feel calmer and I started to try and make some sense out of my situation. First and foremost, I was convinced that it was not my imagination. What I had seen, I had seen. The whole business seemed to be without rational explanation. What was my tormentor trying to achieve? The cut girth was a blatant attempt to do me bodily harm, but what was the sense in this, and why burn those papers? What could anyone hope to gain by those actions? Always I came back to the same two questions. Why? Who? And it was becoming more and more obvious that I should have to answer the second question first, for without knowing who, I doubted if I should ever know why.

Whoever it was must have had some sort of motive, be it real or imaginary. Since, search as I might, I could think of no possible reason, I concluded that either the motive must be imaginary or my enemy must be mad.

If only there was one person in whom I could trust and confide. Letty? Today she had proved that she cared about what happened to me, but anything I said to Letty would most certainly be repeated below stairs. Ormerod, was, of course, a possibility. He already knew about the girth, but somehow, though I know I could count on his sympathy, I could not see that great, earthy, practical man taking this teddy bear business seriously. As for the others, there was only Uncle Joshua of whom I could be absolutely certain, and I was still determined that he should not be presented with any worries which could be kept from him.

It was while I was thinking along those lines that there was a tap on the door.

"Who's there?" I called nervously.

"It's me, coz." It was Henry's voice. "Can I come in?"

It was in that instant that I made a sudden decision. Here was I, a soldier's daughter, behaving like a frightened school girl. I would not avoid them, but I would seek their company and try and draw the enemy's fire. I almost smiled, for the first time that afternoon.

"Coz, are you all right?"

"Sorry, Henry," I called. "Do come in."

Henry entered, his handsome face bearing an expression of concern.

"Emma, I heard that you were not well," he said. "I hope you don't mind, but I wanted to know if there was anything that I could do."

"Why, how thoughtful of you, cousin," I replied. "No, I don't think that there is anything I need."

"But I. . . ." he looked puzzled.

"You've been listening to Dr. Harrison, have you not?" I asked him.

"As a matter of fact, it was Letty who told me."

"Letty is a sweet girl, but she is inclined to exaggerate. I would not advise you to take too much note of what Letty says."

"I see," he said slowly. "And you're sure you are all right and there is nothing I can do for you?"

"There is one thing," I said. "You can tell Barton that I shall be down to dinner."

"But I understood, I mean, Dr. Harrison, didn't she. . . ."

"Dr. Harrison gave me certain advice which I intend to ignore. I am the mistress of this house and in it I shall do as I choose."

Henry seemed utterly nonplussed by my attitude. Probably Letty had dramatized my condition to such an extent that he thought I was really ill. I made up my mind to make things easier for him. After all, if, incredibly, he was my adversary, he would be more likely to reveal himself if he did not feel I suspected.

"Henry, it was very nice of you to leave me that rose," I said. "I am sorry, but I had already promised to have tea with Uncle Josh."

"That was nothing," he said. "You're quite sure that there is nothing wrong?"

"What on earth could be wrong?" I replied. "Now, I am going to ask you to leave, as I must change for dinner."

He left the room and I sank down into my armchair. It had been quite exhausting trying to create a facade of indifference. Inside myself I could feel the tension and fear, but I had to draw my assailant out, if possible, to the point of making him or her strike again. I hoped my enemy, in doing so, would betray himself.

I dressed carefully and went down before the gong had sounded. I wanted to be the first to arrive. In this I succeeded; when I got to the withdrawing room, it was empty. I walked through into the dining room to inspect the table. I was determined that I should give no satisfaction to my ormentor and that I would really start behaving as mistress of Goathlands. When I arrived in the dining room, I found Barton just completing his preparations. The leaves had been removed from the dining table and its two halfround ends formed a perfect circle which would seat, at most, six. On this occasion, it had been laid for four.

"Good evening, Barton," I said. "I will have Mr. Attwood on my right and Mr. Henry on my left."

"Very good, Miss Emma," he replied. "I hope you will pardon my mentioning it, Miss Emma, but I was informed that you had been feeling unwell. I trust that you are now quite recovered?"

"Thank you, Barton, I am feeling much better," I replied.

Having attended to my duties in the dining room, I returned to the withdrawing room. I had only been there a moment or two when I heard the gong sound in the hall. Dr. Harrison came in.

"Really, Miss Waldron, I must protest," she said, coming straight to the point. "I gave you certain advice and you seem to have ignored everything I said. You must understand that I cannot hold myself responsible for—"

"Dr. Harrison," I interrupted her calmly, "I thank you for your concern. As to responsibility, I fully accept that myself, and I quite understand that if I should choose to ignore your advice, I do so entirely at my own risk. Now, shall we say no more about it?"

Her eyes blazed. It was obvious that she was making an effort to control herself. That she had a temper, I knew well. The incident in Uncle Joshua's room had proved that. I looked at the anger in her face. Could she be the one? Perhaps; it was so hard to suspect either of the others. And what could be her motive? Perhaps she feared that my presence at Goathlands might reduce her influence over Uncle Joshua? If she wanted to control my uncle, it would be for a reason known only to herself. If

this was the truth, he really did need me here; it made m
presence in the house even more important.

"I did not want to be forced into this position, Mis
Waldron," she said. "But unless you are sensible and do a
I suggest, I shall be forced to a point where I shall have n
alternative other than to lay the whole matter before you
uncle, even though it may cause him some distress."

This was one thing I could not permit. "Doctor," I re
plied firmly, "I absolutely forbid you to say anything o
this matter. I will not have Sir Joshua worried."

She was clearly very angry at my reply and was about t
say something, but was prevented by the arrival of Henry.

"Good evening, ladies," he said, smiling gaily. "Woul
either of you care for an aperitif?"

"Thank you, we would not," Dr. Harrison declined fo
both of us.

"I will answer for myself, doctor, if you don't mind,"
said coldly.

"Well, coz?" said Henry, smiling that strange crooke
smile of his. "I think it would do you good."

"I will take a very small glass of sherry wine," I said de
fiantly.

"That's new, I must say," said Henry. I do not thin
that Henry had really expected me to take anything.

"I have never known you to take an aperitif," he con
tinued. "Amontillado?"

"Thank you," I said, having no idea what he meant.

It was quite true, I had never taken a drink before a
meal. Underneath my brave exterior there was a ver
frightened little girl trying to get out. I had heard gentle
men remark on occasion that a small quantity of alcoholi
beverage was a help under trying circumstances. I ha
been forced into a situation where I should be able to pu
their theory to the test.

I looked at Henry closely as he handed my glass to me
His smile was not really crooked, more whimsical. No, no

Henry. He, in spite of all his weaknesses, had been so kind and considerate toward me, and had not Uncle Joshua assured me that it was Henry's wish that I should come to Goathlands? If that was true, then he would need to be evil beyond belief to have wanted me here only so that he might destroy me.

"Your health, coz." He raised his glass.

I sipped my sherry wine. I must say that it gave a most pleasant feeling of warmth, though I did not altogether approve of the taste. I glanced towards Doctor Harrison; she sat there grimly, silent and disapproving. Henry seemed, if anything, amused by the situation. I looked round as Roger came into the room.

"Good heavens, Emma," he said, looking at my glass. "You'll get tight. I heard that you were not well, there's nothing serious, is there?"

His last question was directed partially to Dr. Harrison.

"Miss Waldron is being very—"

I stopped the doctor before she could say "foolish." "I suppose that I should feel flattered by all this concern over my health," I remarked. "But I am really quite well and would be grateful if the subject were discussed no further."

"Yes, ma'am," he said with mock meekness. "I hear and obey. Dry sherry, please, Henry."

As Roger got his drink, I took a good look at him. Of all three present, I knew him least well. Yet, I could not help feeling strangely attracted to this seemingly gay, flamboyant man. Henry was in a formal dinner jacket, the sort of thing one would expect, but not Roger. He was wearing a normal dinner suit, but his coat was a deep purple velvet smoking jacket with silk facings and black silk cord embroidery. His hair was just a little too long, and that unruly forelock kept falling across his brow and constantly being pushed back into position. Was it conceivable that this charming overgrown schoolboy was the one?

But then, it is said that the devil himself has infinite charm. I was determined that I should not jump to conclusions. As, sadly, it had to be someone, I should have preferred it to be Dr. Harrison, but that was only because I did not like her, and I must not let personal prejudice color my judgment. I had to keep my resolve, keep a completely open mind and watch and wait.

"I think I am of a mind to go riding tomorrow," I said quite deliberately.

"I doubt if that would be wise, Miss Waldron," said Dr. Harrison.

"Where were you thinking of going?" asked Roger.

"Just around the estate," I replied.

"You'd better be careful if you are going out tomorrow," said Henry. "Ormerod will be burning stubble in the bottom field if the weather holds."

"In that case, it might be nice to ride over and see him," I said.

Further discussion of my proposed ride was halted by the arrival of Barton, who announced that dinner was served. I went over to Roger.

"Would you do me the honor of taking me in?" I asked him.

"It would be a privilege," he replied, offering me his arm.

I laid my hand on his. As I have said before, his were big peasant's hands, strong and firm with skin like sandpaper, quite out of keeping with the rest of his appearance, which was cultured and gentle. As we approached the dining room and Henry and Dr. Harrison stood aside to allow us to precede them, I felt an urge to move closer to Roger than propriety would allow. Of course, I did no such thing. In truth, I found his presence strangely though pleasantly disturbing.

It was almost with regret that I took my hand away and allowed him to seat me. Roger went to his place, Henry mumbled a perfunctory grace, and Barton commenced serving the meal.

When we ladies withdrew after dinner, Dr. Harrison immediately left me. I realized that she had not spoken a word since we had gone in to eat. She must have been very angry with me. I nibbled at a bonbon and poured myself a cup of coffee. I noticed that my hand was trembling slightly as I did this. Though I was quite proud of my performance thus far, I was well aware that it was a performance and that the threat and the fear were still very much there.

I was sitting alone when Roger and Henry, having finished their cigars, came to join me.

"What, no doctor?" asked Roger.

"I don't think she was feeling too well, she retired early," I replied as I poured their coffee.

I handed them their cups, aware that both men were watching me intently. What, I wondered, had they been discussing in there?

"Would you care for a turn around the house before retiring?" Henry asked me.

"I'll come too, if I may," Roger said before I had a chance to reply.

I would have dearly loved to have done that. It was a beautiful night and Goathlands was a very romantic spot on such an evening. I knew that I could not do it; the strain was beginning to tell. Perhaps if Roger had asked me alone?

"Thank you so much," I replied. "It has been a very tiring day and I really feel that I should like to go to bed now, so if you will excuse me. . . ."

We said our good nights, and I left them and went up to my rooms.

When I arrived there, I found Letty busy with warming pans.

"Oh, miss," she said when she saw me. "I'm so glad to see you so much better after your turn."

"Dear Letty," I replied. "You were very good to me today, I shall not forget it, I promise you."

"That's nothing, miss," she said. "Is there anything else I can do for you?"

"Yes," I answered. "There is one thing. Will you be seeing either of the grooms tonight?"

"There's one of them, Arthur, he wants to take me for a walk, miss.'"

"Well, you be careful with your Arthur, Letty," I warned.

"Oh, I haven't decided to go yet."

"Well, it is your business, Letty," I said.

"Not if Mr. Barton catches me it isn't, miss."

"Well, in any case, I want you to give Arthur a message for me." I knew that Ormerod would have gone back to his cottage by that time, so I had to send my instructions to the groom. "Will you tell your Arthur that I shall be riding Honey tomorrow morning, so I should like him to bring him in and groom him before ten o'clock. And tell him to let Mr. Ormerod know."

"I'll do that, miss. Now if Mr. Barton catches me I'll be able to tell him that I'm just delivering a message from the mistress."

"All right, Letty," I said, laughing. "That will be all, except don't bring the morning tea tomorrow, I want to sleep right through."

I had actually laughed. I watched Letty go with a smile; that child was good to me. I should have to make a few discreet inquiries about this Arthur and see if he was good for Letty.

What a day it had been. I think that in the last twelve hours I had been through every emotion I had ever known. Now that I was alone at last, I wondered what the morrow would bring.

I undressed slowly, thinking, I must sit for a while in my dressing gown, before the fire. I locked the outer door and sat down, looking into the flames. It did not work, however. There was no relaxation, and I knew that what I needed most of all was rest. Anyway, I thought, they all knew what I intended to do tomorrow, and I would do it, but I would be on my guard and watching every moment.

Perhaps tomorrow I would discover the identity of my enemy, or perhaps . . . ? But I was not going to think about that.

I went to bed and slept without dream or disturbance.

Chapter Fourteen

THE NEXT MORNING I awoke and stretched my body luxuriously as consciousness came to me. I got out of bed, put on my dressing gown, and opened the curtains. The hands of my bedroom clock pointed to ten o'clock. I had slept for twelve hours. Physically, I felt refreshed and well; the last vestiges of the aches and pains from my fall had gone. Mentally, I felt alert, and my determination to follow my plan was as strong as ever. I was still nervous and had to admit that I was rather frightened at the thought that, by telling everyone what I intended to do today, I had made of myself a willing target. Of course, there was always the other side of the coin: perhaps, for just those reasons, my assailant might decide not to try anything.

As I dressed in my riding habit, once more beautiful thanks to Letty's ministrations, I planned my route. If Ormerod was going to burn the stubble in the bottom field, he would need a breeze from the north or east. As far as I could tell from looking out of my window, he had this. A northeasterly would mean that the fire would travel in the direction of Blawath Beck, where it would burn itself out, thus being quite safe. He would probably light a strip parallel with the stream and about fifteen yards away from the bank. He would burn this first in order to create a fire break. He would then move back and burn off the remaining width of the field in two sections. I decided that I would first ride round the boundary and then watch some of the burning from the top of Northdale Scar.

I left my rooms and made for the dining room, where I found, as I had expected, that breakfast had long been cleared away. I decided that I would go down to the kitchen, as I had so often done as a child, and see what I could wheedle out of Mrs. Jollyman. When I arrived, I found Letty sitting at the big white kitchen table, drinking a cup of tea. She jumped up as I entered.

"Was you looking for me, Miss Emma?" she asked. "I didn't know you was up yet, can I get you anything?"

"It's all right, Letty,"' I replied. "I would like some breakfast, but I think I had better ask cook myself."

I was sufficiently aware of the hierarchy below stairs to realize that asking Letty to produce breakfast for me down there was like asking her to commit high treason.

"Please, miss," she said, "I told Arthur about your horse, miss.'"

"Good, then I expect that it will be ready for me," I said as Mrs. Jollyman came in carrying a basket of vegetables.

"Good morning, Mrs. Jollyman," I greeted her.

"Good morning, Miss Emma," she replied, placing her basket on the table. "And what can we do for you today?"

"I was hoping you might be able to find me a bit to eat. I missed breakfast," I added by way of explanation.

"Slept in, eh?" said Mrs. Jollyman, hands on hips and adopting that expression of mock ferocity which I had learned to ignore at the age of four.

"Yes, I slept in," I answered meekly.

"Shall I bring you something up, miss?" asked Letty.

"You will do no such thing, my girl," snapped Mrs. Jollyman. "Just set a place for your mistress at the table here while I cook her some breakfast."

I watched as, using just one hand, she broke two eggs into the frying pan and placed a thick slice of home cured York ham on the grill. I could see that I was not going to eat any lunch. When we were children, we always had been able to beg a meal off Mrs. Jollyman, but we would feel the sharp edge of her tongue if we should dare to leave any scraps on our plates. I was amused to find that this had been so bred into me that I knew that whatever Mrs. Jollyman placed before me, I would eat in its entirety. A mug of strong tea and a thick slice of freshly baked bread and butter completed my breakfast.

Feeling somewhat overfed, I thanked Mrs. Jollyman and left the house in the direction of the stables.

The big barn was open when I arrived there, and Kittiwake was standing outside. Roger was sitting in the cockpit with a row of tools laid out in front of him. He hailed me as I was passing.

"Just going, or have you been?" he asked.

"Just got out of bed," I replied.

"Lucky you," he replied. "I've been at this since eight and I daren't stop; look." He pointed in the direction of the house.

I was just able to make out a shape at Uncle Joshua's window. I waved in his direction, and he waved back in reply.

"Which way are you going?" asked Roger.

"Round the boundary to Northdale Scar. I'll watch the burning from there and then come home," I replied.

"I might wander out in that direction and meet you after I have finished here," said Roger.

"Are you going to ride?" I asked.

"No, no, I think I shall walk," he answered.

"Well, I must get along," I said. "Where is Basil?"

"You're all right going through the barn," replied Roger. "He's in his kennel. He wouldn't touch you anyway, he's all bark and no bite."

"Thanks, but I'll wait until I know him better before I take any chances with him."

I carried on to the stables, where I found Arthur waiting for me.

"I saw you coming, miss. Shall I tack up Honey? He's all ready," said Arthur.

I told him to go ahead, and he disappeared into Honey's loose box. He seemed to be rather a long time, so I went over to the box and looked in. Arthur was looking at the leathers under the saddle flap.

"What are you doing, Arthur?" I asked.

"Sorry to be so long, miss, but Mr. Ormerod told me that I was not to hand the horse over to you until I had inspected every inch of tack and every stitch."

I was glad to hear that Ormerod was not taking any chances.

"He told me that if you had an accident he would beat the living daylights out of me," concluded Arthur.

He led Honey out. I pulled the girth up another hole, and Arthur led him over to the mounting block. It seemed that the privilege of giving me a leg up was reserved to Ormerod alone.

I mounted and was just about to move off when Arthur interrupted me.

"Excuse me, miss, I almost forgot. Mr. Ormerod asked me to give you this." He handed me an apple.

Dear Ormerod, he had thought of everything. Honey, being the creature he was, was quite aware of this transaction and of its implications. He stretched his head back toward me and started to turn in a tight left hand circle, no doubt hoping to catch up with himself. I knew that I should not have given the apple to him then, but I did. I had the feeling that it would probably be much easier to accede to Honey's request than to spend the next hour arguing about it. He munched the apple while I sat waiting; he managed to drop half. Arthur retrieved it and informed me that I was spoiling Honey.

The pre-ride ritual having been completed to Honey's satisfaction, we set off down Howl Moor in the direction of Nelly Ayre Fosse, retracing our steps of Wednesday. As I rode along at a brisk trot, I began to feel free again. It was marvelous to feel the cool autumn breeze in my hair, and to breathe in the beautiful clean smell of the clear Yorkshire air, which was spiced with just the faintest tang of the sea. Both of these things helped me to relax and to enjoy my ride.

After about half an hour of trotting and cantering, I arrived at a point a mile or so east of the house. Here I left my previous route and headed southwesterly in the direction of Crag Stone Rigg. Crag Stone Rigg is the hill due south of Goathlands that terminates in a gully, followed by a short climb up to the top of Northdale Scar. The Scar itself is a sheer cliff, some thirty feet high and perhaps half a mile long, overlooking the wheat fields toward Blawath Beck.

As I rode in the direction of Northdale Scar, I could see the smoke rising from the fields in the distance. Honey took me down into the gully and then up again toward the cliff edge. The panorama which spread out before us as we mounted the crest was quite a dramatic sight.

I slowed Honey to a walk as we approached the top of the Scar. I could see Ormerod away to the right, inside an elbow formed by Blawath Beck. I could see that he was busy. He had another man with him, and they were walking down each end of the line of burning stubble, making sure that the fire was contained and that it did not spread beyond the boundaries of the field. The rest of the view from the top of Northdale Scar is quite magnificent. To the south is the expanse of Pickering Forest, behind you stands Goathlands, to the west lie the rolling moors, and to the east there is a single-track railway line which skirts both Lockton High Moor and the strangely titled Snod Hill.

I walked Honey almost to the cliff edge and then stopped. I leaned forward to pat his neck and give him permission to crop a little of the grass on which he was standing. I let the reins go loose and he lowered his head, carefully selecting the most succulent tufts. I doubt if he enjoyed it very much; there had been so little rain in recent weeks that the grass was very dry. I realized that this was giving Ormerod and his assistant quite a lot of extra work, as they were constantly beating out the fire at the ends of the line in order to prevent it from spreading. They were so intent on their task that I am quite sure that they never noticed me.

I had been sitting there for some ten or fifteen minutes, watching the men working and enjoying the view, when I suddenly became aware of the smell of smoke. At first this meant little to me; after all, I was watching the fire in the field. Then Honey lifted his head and, laying his ears flat, started to shiver. I began to realize that the smoke I was smelling could not possibly be coming from the fire I was watching. The breeze, light though it was, was coming from behind me. I was beginning to feel worried as I looked back in the direction of the house. To my horror, I saw smoke rising from the gully behind me.

I urged Honey in the direction of the smoke, but he would not move. There was no time to be gentle with him, as the smoke seemed to be coming from a very wide area. I laid into him with my whip but it had no effect. He was standing stock still, trembling with fear.

Quickly I dismounted and ran toward the gully, and as I did so I was appalled to see that there was fire on either side of me. I ran to the top of the dip, and there the full implications of my situation became all too apparent. We were completely cut off by an arc of fire which spread from the edge of the cliff to the right, on through the gully, and round to the cliff edge on the left.

I was sure that at that moment I could have run through the fire to safety, but could I abandon Honey? Horses are remarkably stupid in the presence of fire. How often did one read stories of their being burned to death in their stalls simply because they refused to run out of a blazing stable? Honey was no exception. I knew that he would stand there transfixed and be terribly burned, perhaps even to death, before he would attempt to make a move; the sight of the smoke and flames seemed to paralyze him.

The situation was rapidly becoming critical. At its nearest point, the fire was only some ten or twelve yards away. Thank the Lord the breeze is light, I thought, for I knew that a sudden gust of wind might envelop me and Honey in an inferno of flame. I searched frantically for a way out as fingers of flame probed out in our direction from the main body of the fire. Suddenly, I saw what might be a chance to my left. There was a flat rock outcrop, almost circular and about seven or eight feet in diameter. The fire would not be able to burn on that. If only I could get Honey there, we might be able to get through as the fire swept round. I rushed over to my horse and tugged with all my strength at his reins.

"Honey," I cried. "Honey, don't make me leave you. I'll have to if you don't move. Please, Honey, please."

The tears were streaming down my face as I begged and pleaded with him, but he just stood there, ears back and eyes rolling, his beautiful body shivering in some sort of diabolical anticipation as the flames crept nearer.

By this time, sparks were landing all round us and I realized that I was going to have to leave him if I was to get to the flat rock and have any sort of a chance myself.

"Goodbye, Honey, I can do no more," I said between my sobs.

I tried one last time to move him and then, just as I was about to leave him and make for the rock, I screamed as a smouldering figure burst through the wall of fire and rolled on the ground, furiously beating out the sparks on his clothing. It was Roger.

"Roger, I. . . ."

"Shut up and get on the horse," he shouted.

"He won't move," I cried.

"Don't argue," he roared, picking me up bodily and thrusting me onto the saddle.

"Over there," I said, pointing to my rock.

He was stripping off his jacket and then his shirt.

"Put this over your head," he commanded, pushing the jacket into my hands.

I took the jacket and saw that he was binding the shirt over Honey's eyes.

"Get that thing over your head," he yelled at me. "You don't want to burn that lovely face."

He took hold of the reins and, talking to him gently all the while, led Honey to the rock. Honey, now blind, was moving as obediently as a child.

"Now, listen to me," said Roger. "I am going to wait until the fire is almost surrounding us and then I shall make a dash for it, so hang on tight. If the horse stops, get down and run. Do you understand?"

"Yes," I replied.

"Keep the jacket over your head. There is no sense in risking getting your face or eyes burned. After all, we only need one pair of eyes to get us through."

"I want to tell you. . . ."

"Shut up and do what I say. You can tell me afterwards," he snapped.

I buried my head in the jacket and waited in the blackness for what seemed an eternity, seeing nothing and feeling only the occasional shiver as it ran through Honey's body.

"Now get hold of his mane. Hold tight. Now!"

Suddenly we were moving forward at a trot. I don't know how long it took, but it could only have been a matter of seconds. I felt Honey shy once, but without stopping his forward motion, and then I could feel him descending into the gully. We stopped and I pulled the coat from over my head. Roger was standing smiling at me.

"There," he said. "That wasn't too bad, was it?"

"Oh, Roger," I cried. "How can I ever thank you?"

"You could have got out of it," he said.

"But I couldn't move Honey," I replied. "And I couldn't bear the thought of leaving him."

"You're very fond of that animal, aren't you?" he said.

I nodded silently as I handed him his coat.

"Yes," I whispered. "Very fond. Here, you had better put this on, it is getting quite chilly."

"Why in heaven's name did you come out there when you knew that they were burning stubble?" he asked as he slipped into his jacket.

"But I didn't," I cried. "What I mean is, Ormerod is down there at the beck. They're burning the bottom field. I was watching them."

"You mean that all of this was started by accident?" he said, looking at the line of the fire which was by now burning itself out along the cliff edge.

"I hope so," I replied, aware of the incredulity in his tone.

Dear God, this could be yet another attempt. I shuddered at at the thought.

"Look here, you are cold," said Roger. "Why don't you ride up to the house and get warm?"

"No, I'm not cold," I said quickly. "You think it might not have been an accident?"

"It must have been started by someone," he replied. "But if they had started it accidentally, what I can't understand is how they failed to see you and warn you."

"Did you see anyone on your way here?" I asked.

"Yes, I saw someone on a horse, but they were over toward Snod Hill."

"Man or woman?" I asked.

"That I couldn't say. They were too far away and riding hard. Knowing that you were going out, I thought that it might be you. Getting back to this fire, you obviously think that it might have been deliberate."

"I'm not sure," I said.

The feeling was growing within me all the time that this had indeed been another attack. If this was so, I had not altogether failed in my plan. Though I could still not be sure of the identity of whoever was doing this to me, I felt that I could now eliminate Roger.

"Well," he said gravely, "we'll soon find out." He paused. "That is, if you want to find out."

Did I want to? I so dearly wanted to prove by some miracle that it had been an accident. But the truth, however frightening, was essential. Ignorance or knowledge, providing either is complete, I could deal with. Uncertainty would drive me mad.

"Yes," I replied. "I must find out."

"Come on then."

I dismounted, and we tied Honey to a bush where he could graze contentedly. Roger led me to the cliff edge where the burnt grass started. It was still smoldering and crackling in places, but by now it was quite safe. Roger's eyes were fixed on the ground as we walked along the bottom of the gully. He told me that he doubted very much that there would be any visible tracks, as the ground was too hard and rocky, but he kept on looking. After about fifteen minutes, the gully shallowed to a narrow dip. At this point the line of the fire swung abruptly towards the cliff edge. As we approached this point, we became aware of a small column of smoke rising fron what, at a distance, appeared to be a small shrub or bush. As we drew nearer, the object in question took the form of a shapeless bundle. Roger ran on ahead to examine it. I followed him, and when I caught him up he was looking very grave.

"Look at this," he said.

It was a bundle of charred and almost burnt-out hay. It had been bound with wire, and there were about ten or twelve feet of rope attached to the wire.

When I arrived, Roger was holding the end of the rope, examining it carefully. He dropped the rope and came toward me, his gray eyes more serious than I had ever seen them before. He held out his hands toward me and took both of mine in his.

"What is it?" I asked, frightened by his serious manner.

"Emma." He spoke very quietly. "Someone tried to kill you."

Chapter Fifteen

THERE WAS A long silence.

"Emma," said Roger, "do you understand what I said to you? Someone is trying to kill you. This was a deliberate act."

"Yes, I know," I said quietly.

"Someone made this," he said, indicating the still smoldering bundle. "They lit it and dragged it through the dry grass in that gully and tried to cut you off against the cliff edge."

"Roger, will you take me back to the house? I'll walk with you, I don't want to be alone."

"Of course I will," he replied. "Then I shall go straight to the police. This is a matter for them to deal with."

"No, not the police," I pleaded. "Please don't go to the police."

For the second time someone wanted to take my troubles to the police, and for the second time I felt that I could not permit it. The same reasons still applied as when Ormerod had made the same suggestion about the broken girth.

"Why on earth not?" said Roger. "That is a very foolish idea. Someone deliberately tried to endanger your life. I cannot see that we have any alternative."

"Roger, I beg you, please not the police, Uncle Josh. . . ."

"If you are worrying about your uncle, you can stop right now," he interrupted. "He's a tough old bird. No one knows that better than I do. As soon as he hears about this I am sure that he will insist on the police being called in."

"But there is no reason for him to hear about it," I said.

"Emma." Roger spoke very firmly. "He has got to know about it. If you will not tell him, then I shall. I am not joking, and it is no good arguing with me. I insist on him knowing."

I was defeated. Roger meant what he said. I sensed a will of iron in the man standing before me, but if Uncle Josh had to be told, then I had to be the one to tell him.

"Look here," I said, "I'll make a bargain with you. If I promise to tell Uncle Joshua, will you, for your part, promise me that you will not go to the police unless he agrees?"

"When will you tell him? Today? I will not wait longer."

"I shall tell him this afternoon and let you know what he says at dinner," I replied.

"I don't approve of waiting," said Roger. "But I agree. Provided that you keep your side of the bargain, I shall not act without your permission. But, if for any reason at all you fail, then I shall go to the police this evening."

"Thank you," I replied. "I'll agree to that."

I realized that he had gone as far as he would. We walked on in silence for a while. I found it very comforting to have this strong, purposeful man beside me. I had a feeling of security and relaxation in his company. How I wanted to tell him everything that had happened, but I realized that if I did that, I could no longer control events. I knew that I would find myself submitting to his will. I looked at him, strong and purposeful, his jacket open over his bare chest. He had discarded his shirt after ripping it off Honey.

"I really am grateful for everything you have done," I said. "And I'm sorry about your shirt. I feel that I should replace it for you."

"I tell you what," he said. "I have a better idea. Instead of giving me a new shirt, why don't you come fishing with me?"

"But it is the closed season," I said. Salmon fishing finished at the beginning of October.

"Oh dear me, no. Not salmon," he replied. "I haven't the patience for river fishing. I've got a small coble which I keep at Whitby. I'll go out first thing tomorrow morning and sail it round to Robin Hood's Bay. You could get Ormerod to drive you out about eleven, by which time I should be waiting for you. Well, what do you say?"

"I should love to come," I answered.

I found the thought of spending a morning in his company most attractive. I suggested that I might ask Mrs. Jollyman to prepare a picnic hamper so that we could stay out all day if the weather was good. We could get home in the early evening and cook our catch for supper. I was warming to this man in a manner which I could only describe as pleasantly disturbing.

By this time, we had arrived at the stables. There we found that Ormerod had got back before us. He came toward us looking full of concern as he observed that I was dismounted.

"Has anything happened?" he asked, and there was an ominous ring to his voice.

"No," replied Roger. "I met Miss Waldron on the moor and we walked back together. Have you just returned?"

"Not more than ten minutes ago, sir," he answered.

"Can you tell me if anyone other than Miss Waldron has had a horse out this morning?"

I could tell that he was trying to make the inquiry sound casual.

"That I wouldn't know, Mr. Attwood," said Ormerod. "I've been out myself since about half past seven. There was only Arthur left up here, and he's gone. I understand that Dr. Harrison sent him to Pickering to get some supplies."

My heart missed a beat when Ormerod mentioned Dr. Harrison's name.

"Well, do you know if any of the horses have been out, apart from Honey?" Roger asked.

"Well, there were three to be brought in this morning," replied Ormerod. "Arthur went in a horseless carriage, so he hasn't taken one. The other two were Mr. Henry's mare and my cob, they should still be in their stalls. Just what is it thou are after, Mr. Attwood, if I might be so bold?"

"Let's go and look at them," said Roger, ignoring Ormerod's question. "Can your man there take Honey?"

Ormerod beckoned the groom, who took Honey from me and led him toward his box.

"Mr. Henry's mare is in there," said Ormerod, indicating a loose box.

When we looked in, the big black mare was munching away contentedly at her hay. I still did not understand what it was that Roger had in mind, but he did seem to have some definite sort of plan. He looked the mare over carefully and seemed satisfied.

"And the cob?" he asked Ormerod.

"First box round the corner," replied Ormerod.

We went to the cob's box, and it was when we saw him that I realized what Roger was looking for. The animal's neck and withers were foam-flecked; he was covered with sweat and steaming. That horse had been ridden, ridden very recently and very hard. Ormerod was furious.

"Who the devil's left him in this condition?" he roared. "Just wait until I get hold of that Arthur, he'll need to have a right good explanation for this."

"I doubt very much if Arthur will be able to tell you anything," said Roger. "What I would like you to do, Ormerod, is to see if there is any way you can find out who it was that took your horse out. Do you think you could?"

"I can look at the tack," said Ormerod.

"What will that tell you?" I asked.

"If it's warm, it's been used, it'll be in a mess too from the look of the horse. If it's a side saddle, it were a lady."

"And if it was a man's saddle, would you be sure that it was a man?" asked Roger.

"Not for certain," said Ormerod. "There are ladies who I have known to ride astride, though I cannot say as I hold with such practices, immodest I reckon."

"Have you ever seen any lady here riding astride?" I asked.

"I recall seeing Dr. Harrison do it once. Of course, she's different, being a lady doctor and all that."

Ormerod obviously regarded a lady doctor as some sort of freak who could not be expected to conform to his own high moral standards.

"Thank you, Ormerod," said Roger. "Let me know what you find, anyway. I shall be in the big barn all afternoon."

Ormerod looked hard at me. "There is something wrong, Miss Emma. Is it anything thou can tell me about?"

"No, Ormerod," I replied. "I can't, I'm sorry."

"Thou hast only to say the word," he said.

I was grateful; I knew only too well how I could count on Ormerod. I promised him that the moment there was anything that he could do, I would let him know. I took the opportunity of asking him if he would be able to drive me over to Robin Hood's Bay next morning. He seemed delighted, and we arranged to meet at ten. With that, Roger and I took our leave as he headed toward the tack room, no doubt to proceed with his investigations.

I walked with Roger as far as the big barn, where I left him and continued toward the house. Once again I needed to be alone in order to take stock of my situation.

It appeared that, for the first time, my knowledge had progressed. Even if I were to leave aside all personal feelings and desires, I felt that I could now be morally certain that, whoever it might be, Roger was certainly not my tormentor. It thrilled me as I thought back, almost with pleasure, to the moment when his form had come crashing through the smoke to my rescue. The masterly way in which he had taken command of the situation, with never a thought for his own safety, had left me feeling—and here I must confess it—more than a little fondness toward him. Why, even at that moment, I could feel the color flushing to my cheeks as I looked back over the events of the morning and forward to the thought of spending the greater part of the morrow in his company.

It was not that I did not still feel nervous. The tension was still there. I found myself continuously glancing over my shoulder to make sure that I was not being followed. I approached every corner with a feeling of trepidation, and when I got to my rooms, I paused at the door, fearful of what it might be hiding from my view.

My fears proved groundless. I went in and washed carefully, for I could still smell the smoke about my person, a nagging reminder of the ordeal to which I had just been submitted. I changed into a day dress of pale blue wool and set off in the direction of Uncle Joshua's rooms.

I was not looking forward to the coming interview. I could not make up my mind where I would begin or how I could phrase myself without making the whole affair appear either too melodramatic or too insignificant. Then there was the question of how much I should tell him. I could not be certain that to tell him all would be the right thing to do, yet I realized that I had to tell him something. I suppose that I could have stuck to my original intention and said nothing at all. I did not regard the promise that I had made to Roger as binding; after all, it had been made under considerable duress. On the other hand, what would happen if I maintained my silence? Roger had left me in no doubt that he would tell Uncle Joshua the entire story and go to the police. He had threatened to do this, and there was no reason to assume that he would fail to carry out his threat. And yet, I argued with myself, it was quite possible that Roger was right. Just suppose that something terrible had happened this morning, or tomorrow morning, or the day after? I shuddered at the thought; it was not very pleasant to contemplate, but it was very real and had to be faced. If a tragedy were to occur, would not the effect on Uncle Joshua be altogether too devastating? Might it not be that he would be incapable of surviving the shock? On balance, perhaps it was better that he should know and be in a position to take whatever action he might deem necessary. Uncle Joshua had always been a man of action, and though his body had been cruelly scarred, the spirit which lived on inside that battered shell was still the same. Above all, I knew he cared for me and trusted me. Could I hope to retain that trust if he were to find out from other sources that I had, by my silence, spurned his trust and denied his protection? I felt trapped. I had to tell him, if only because I knew that he held me so dear.

By the time I had arrived at his rooms, my mind was made up, though I still paused before knocking. I felt again the fear, though for different reasons, which I had felt the first time that I had stood at that threshold. For a moment I hoped that he would not be there or would have some reason for being unable to see me. But these were foolish fears. I raised my hand and knocked at the door.

"Enter."

How the sound of Uncle Josh's voice sent a shiver down my spine. I went in and saw to my dismay that Dr. Harrison was there in the room with him. By that time, I was becoming more and more afraid of that woman. She stood there, tall, expressionless, and statuesque. Her black hair and dress accentuated the pallid, unemotional face which they framed. Her eyes, like black coals of fire, seemed to be delving deep into my mind.

As for Uncle Joshua, he was wearing neither his patch nor his skull cap, and the sight of the poor scarred features made me doubt the wisdom of the course I had chosen. As I looked at his face and remembered my own ordeal by fire, I trembled at the thought of what my own fate might have been but for Roger's timely arrival.

"How very convenient of you to arrive at just this moment, Miss Waldron," Dr. Harrison was speaking. "I was on the point of sending you a message. Would you mind coming over to my rooms for a moment?"

I certainly had no intention of allowing myself to be alone with her, but it was not going to be easy to refuse her while Uncle Joshua was present.

"I . . . I must first talk with my uncle," I said. "There is a matter of some urgency. . . ."

"Can it not wait?" she asked coldly.

"No," I replied. "It is a very private matter and I must talk with him now."

"I doubt if it can be all that urgent," she said, going toward the door. "I think it might be better if you talked to me first."

I made no move.

"All right, Susan," said Uncle Josh. "I'll have a word with Emma first, and then she can come over to you."

I observed with something approaching disgust that he referred to her by her first name.

"Just as you wish, Sir Joshua," she replied. "I shall wait for you, Miss Waldron."

I was relieved to see that she still retained a formal manner of address when speaking to my uncle. I watched her go and wondered if I was, in fact, jealous of the attention he paid to her and she to him.

"Now then, Emma," said Uncle Joshua as soon as we were alone. "What is this thing which cannot wait?"

How I wished that I had asked Roger to come with me. In that moment, I really needed his strength. And there was something else. Was I mistaken, or did I detect a certain coolness in Uncle Joshua's tone?

"Do you mind if I sit down?" I asked. "What I have to say is not going to be easy."

"I'm sorry," he replied. "Do forgive me."

He indicated a chair by the fire, and I sat down and waited while he took the seat facing me.

"Now then, out with it," he said.

"It's awfully difficult to know just where to begin," I replied.

"Emma," he said, "there is only one place to begin, and that is the beginning. I suggest that you try starting there."

"It all started with my teddy bear," I said and then stopped.

A teddy bear, it sounded too utterly ridiculous. I do not know what reaction I espected from Uncle Joshua; incredulity, amazement, even laughter. What I most certainly did not expect was the reaction which I did in fact get.

"Yes," he replied very seriously. "I know."

He knew! The words struck me like a whiplash. How did he know? What did he know? From whence came his knowledge? Or was *he* the moving force behind all of this? No. I put the thought out of my head as soon as it entered; not Uncle Josh, that could never be true.

"Uncle," I said, "how do you know?"

"I was told," he replied.

"By whom?"

"By Dr. Harrison."

The doctor again, always the doctor. I was becoming more and more convinced that this was my enemy. If only I could find a motive. But once again the question burned into me: what reason could she possibly have?

"Dr. Harrison is very worried about you and, quite rightly, approached me on the matter. She told me of the occasion when you came to her in great distress and asked her to come to your room where you showed her a teddy bear lying on your bed."

"Was that all she told you?" I asked.

"I felt it was quite sufficient for me to ask her to make a thorough examination of you and report back to me," said Uncle Joshua.

"But she didn't tell you anything else?"

"Was there more?"

What was I to say? His attitude was one of patient sympathy, and yet I could not go through with it, not then. I would have to wait until I had a chance to talk with Roger. Maybe I could get him to come along with me and tell Uncle Josh about that morning.

I knew that if I was to try and tell him anything now, he

simply would not believe me. And why should he? Like a fool, I had destroyed the only piece of solid evidence that I possessed: the burnt papers.

I made my excuses to him and explained that I would be unable to go and see Dr. Harrison that afternoon but would come over and see her some time the following day. I had to talk with Roger before I did anything.

Surprisingly, Uncle Josh let me go and promised to convey my message to the doctor. In somewhat of a daze, I made my way to my rooms and locked myself in. I sat down and gazed into the fire. Uncle Josh had spoken to me as if I were a child. He had agreed to my request regarding Dr. Harrison without a murmur. He knew about the teddy bear. What was in his mind? What did he imagine was in my mind?

I could think of only one answer to that question. Uncle Joshua thought I was going mad.

Chapter Sixteen

FOR THE FIRST time since my arrival at Goathlands, I had a disturbed night. I went to bed early but found that sleep evaded me. I tossed and turned, dozing fitfully, for how many hours I do not know, but I can remember seeing the dawn and watching it etch its gray lines of light along the edges of the curtains. My mind was in a turmoil. I found it impossible to control my wandering thoughts and relax into the sweet oblivion of sleep. Having decided to tell Uncle Joshua, I had then, through circumstances over which I had no control, been denied the chance. It had been like a blow in the face. I had, I believed, taken very real risks in staying on at Goathlands, and my only reason had been solicitude for my uncle. To find now that he did not trust me was a most shattering experience.

Thank heavens for Roger. In him I had found a friend, maybe something even more, but nonetheless a friend with broad shoulders where I could lay part of the burden of my fears.

Morning could not have come too soon for me. As soon as it was light, I dressed warmly and went downstairs. There was a stillness about the house which was in sharp contrast to the light and bustle of the kitchen as Mrs. Jollyman fussed over the preparations of breakfast and morning trays. If she was surprised to see me, she did not show it; not that I expected her to. I am quite sure that if there had been an earthquake, Mrs. Jollyman would have continued unperturbed with her preparations for the next meal.

I had it in mind to catch Roger before he left and ride over to Whitby with him, but when I inquired, Mrs. Jollyman told me that he had been in an hour earlier, breakfasted, and gone on his way.

Not wanting to face any other members of the household, I asked Mrs. Jollyman if I could again have breakfast in the kitchen and was promptly rewarded with a plate of steaming kidneys. Letty came in to get my tray and was amazed to find me there. However, she refused to be denied her task of looking after me and fussed over me like a mother hen while I ate my breakfast. I was quite glad she had appeared, for I had forgotten the field glasses that Colonel Willoughby had so kindly given me. I thought it would be a good idea to take them with me, so I asked Letty to slip up to my room and get them, cautioning her to tell no one where I was. This seemed to please her, for she left on her errand in a most conspiratorial manner. My main reason in thus cautioning her had, of course, been my desire to avoid any contact with Dr. Harrison before I had had the chance to talk to Roger.

I must have hung around the kitchen for a couple of hours or more. For the greater part of that time, I sat at the white deal table, sipping cups of coffee. The silence was broken by occasional conversations with Mrs. Jollyman about routine matters of running the house. I tried very hard to make everything appear normal, for I was aware that my presence there must have seemed strange to them. However, if anyone was surprised, no one remarked on it.

At a quarter to ten I felt that it would be safe to go over to the stables and meet Ormerod. I was about to leave when Mrs. Jollyman presented me with a wicker picnic box, telling me that Roger had asked her to make it up and give it to me before I left. So, armed with my binoculars and the picnic box, I left the house by the servants' entrance.

When I got to the stable yard, I found Ormerod fiddling with one of Uncle Joshua's horseless carriages.

"Morning, Miss Emma," he greeted me. "Thou's a mite early."

"I know I am," I replied. "But I was ready, so I thought you wouldn't mind if I came over to meet you."

"Bless thee, no," he said, smiling and then looking at me with a touch of concern in his face. "Art thou well? Thou seemest a little pale this morning."

"I am sure that there is nothing wrong with me that a breath of North Sea air will not cure," I said, with an attempt at a gaiety that I did not feel.

"Right then," he replied. "We might as well be off. I'll take that." He indicated the picnic basket.

He put the basket into the back seat and then proceeded to wind the handle that jutted from the front of the contraption. There were a couple of coughs and splutters, but apart from them, nothing happened.

"It'll be right in a minute," said Ormerod optimistically. He went round to the driving seat and adjusted some of the little levers which seemed to grow in profusion around the steering wheel.

I was glancing anxiously back toward the house, worried in case anyone had noticed my absence and come looking for me. To my relief, there was no one in sight except Arthur, who was carrying buckets into one of the loose boxes.

Ormerod was winding his handle again. Suddenly there was a loud bang and a puff of obnoxious smoke, and the machine rattled into life.

"Right," Ormerod shouted into my ear. "I'll give thee a hand up."

I clambered aboard the clanking, hissing, shaking thing. Ormerod ran round and jumped into the driving seat, and with a rattle and a roar, we were off.

In order to get onto the main drive, which ran across Howl Moor to the road at Nelly Ayre Fosse, we had to skirt the big barn to the front of the house and then turn straight down the drive past the summer house. As we were passing the house, I looked up, and what I saw sent a chill shiver down my spine. There at one of the upper windows stood Dr. Harrison, staring tight-lipped in my direction.

We followed our usual route as far as Goathland Village, and after leaving it behind, started up Sleights Moor. The road climbs sharply away from Ellen Beck Ford until, by the time you are in the middle of the moor, you are nearly a thousand feet up.

It was from here, after snorting and spluttering and bumping up the hill, that I saw the North Sea for the first time since my arrival. Though the coast was still some six miles distant, I could just make out the curve of the cliffs overlooking Robin Hood's Bay, and away to the left, the busy little fishing port of Whitby.

What happy times I had spent there as a child, when my parents or Uncle Josh and Aunt Hester would take Cousin Henry and myself for a day at the seaside. I was sure that somewhere around the house we still had the collection of beautiful sea shells which we had so carefully garnered from the tidal pools among the rocks beneath Ness Point.

Ahead lay all those happy childhood memories. I looked back; I could still see Goathlands standing four-square on top of its hill. What lay there? The house itself had taken on an air of menace toward me. All of its friendliness seemed to have vanished; now the shadows which it cast in the autumn sunlight were shadows over my life, shadows from which I desperately wanted to escape. Ahead, however, all was clear and clean and bright. I tried to picture Roger as he sailed his little boat round from Whitby harbor; I could almost see him in my mind's eye as he handled his craft with ease and skill. Of course, I was fantasizing. I had no means of knowing whether Roger was a good sailor, but he was so efficient and practical in all he turned his hand to that I was quite sure that he was equally skilled in the art of sailing.

I looked at Ormerod and wondered whether he intended to accompany us on our fishing trip. I knew that he should, even though nothing had been said, it being hardly proper for me to go out alone in a boat with a man. Secretly, I hoped that he would not come with us, and I could not help feeling a little disloyal at the thought. It occurred to me that I could quite easily ask him about his intentions, but the clattering and bumping, just as in our ride from Malton, put paid to any attempt at conversation.

We rattled down the hill toward Little Beck, and the sea disappeared from view. Then we were climbing again over Fylingdale's Moor. Soon the sea reappeared, this time to stay, as it was now all downhill from the top of the moor to Robin Hood's Bay. I could just make out a number of dots lying about a mile off Ness Point. Their sails were

down, and I supposed them to be the Whitby cobles waiting for the slack water between tides when the fish always
seem to feed. Far out toward the horizon was a beautiful
sight: a big three-master was plowing her way north under
full sail. I tried to look at these sights through my field
glasses, but the vibration was such that I found it impossible either to focus or to hold them steady.

At last we arrived at the cliff top, and Ormerod stopped
the motor. The silence was wonderful, broken only by the
mewing of the kittiwakes as they went their graceful ways,
landing and taking off from the rocks beneath us.

"Beautiful, isn't it, Miss Emma?" said Ormerod.

He was taking a pair of long waders from the back of
the motor car. I observed this with a touch of dismay. So
he was coming.

"I gather you are coming with us?" I said.

He observed me with a twinkle in his eye.

"Well, miss, that's not easy to say," he said, in a tone
that I can only describe as devious. "Of course, I have to
come out with you, that's only proper."

"Yes, I suppose so," I replied without enthusiasm.

"And I brought these waders along because someone is
going to have to push the boat out, and moreover, I'll be
able to put thee aboard without thee getting wet."

"Yes?" I said, for he obviously had not finished.

"Well, Miss Emma," he continued. "After I get thee
aboard, I go round and give the coble a mighty heave, I'm
pretty strong thou knows, and I might just push that coble
so far that I'm not able to get in myself." He grinned at
me.

"Ormerod, you are very wicked," I replied, smiling.
"But thank you."

"Now, miss, if I'm going to do this we'd better wait up
here until Mr. Attwood has got her properly beached, otherwise it might be too easy and we might both end up in
the boat."

How sweet of him, I thought, but then Ormerod always seemed to know how I felt about everything.

As I looked out over the water to see if I could catch sight of Roger, a slight wave of nausea swept over my body, so I sat down on the grass near the cliff edge. I supposed that the tensions of the last few days and the lack of sleep last night had left me feeling fairly fragile both in mind and body. However, I was not going to worry. I was pretty sure that I would feel much better once I got out onto the sea with Roger.

I scanned the water through my glasses, and just rounding Ness Point I picked up a small red coble under sail. It had a single occupant.

"Ormerod," I called, "do you know the color of Mr. Attwood's boat?"

"Red, miss," replied Ormerod. "Can you see him?"

"He's just rounded Ness Point," I replied.

"Then he'll be some time yet," said Ormerod, who had begun to tinker about inside the engine of the motor car.

So, that was Roger in the little red boat. I could see the spot for which he was making, and as he was having to tack, sailing into the offshore breeze, I estimated that it would take him at least a quarter of an hour to get there. I was quite glad of this, as it gave me time to relax before descending the wooden steps which zigzagged their way down the cliff face.

I watched the boat for a while until I could recognize Roger. He did not look up at all. He seemed intent on managing his sail and bringing his craft into the beach, where he would, no doubt, run her onto the soft sand.

Soon the nausea passed, and I started to enjoy the view. I looked around the bay and tried to pick up familiar detail. It was while I was doing this that, just to the right of the spot for which Roger was making, I saw the seal. It was a very young seal, for there were still quite large patches of brown fur among the adult gray. It was lying

half in and half out of a small pool among the rocks, its
head swaying slightly as it seemed to watch the approaching coble. I wondered whether or not it would stay there
when Roger got close. I assumed that if the seal stayed
where it was, Roger could not miss seeing it.

Roger had now sailed past the point where the seal lay
and was coming about so that he could sail up to the
beach with the wind on his port side. The seal seemed to
watch him as he turned the boat to pass the rocks for the
second time. I turned round to tell Ormerod that Roger
was nearly in, but he seemed to be very busy with the
motor, so I did not disturb him.

Looking back to the shore, I saw that Roger had by
then passed the rocks and that the seal was still there.
Roger dropped his sail and grabbed the tiller, pointing the
boat directly toward the sand. In a moment he had
grounded with his bows well clear of the water. It must
have been just about low tide, and the water had become
so calm that there was no risk of the boat drifting out.

Roger leapt out over the bow, and it was than that I realized that he had seen the seal. He made his way slowly
in the direction of the rock where the animal lay. The seal
had seen his approach and put its head down as though
trying to appear as part of the rock on which it sat. I wondered at the time why it was that it made no attempt to
escape to the sea, which was only a few yards away.

Roger was now on his hands and knees, creeping very
slowly toward the seal. Though Roger could not have been
more than three yards from it, still the seal did not move.
Even when Roger stood up, it made no attempt whatsoever to get away.

Roger walked quite deliberately to where the seal was
lying. He seemed to be examining it; I think he even
touched it as he moved around it. The seal lay there quite
motionless.

Suddenly, Roger straightened up and made his way back to the sand and started to walk up the beach. When he reached the high water line, marked by its usual collection of seaweed and flotsam, he stopped and started to follow it. What could he be doing, I wondered. I had thought him to be on his way to the stairs, but that was obviously not his intention. I suppose that at that point I should have called Ormerod and started down, but I was so intrigued by Roger's actions that I did not think of moving.

Roger stopped, picked something up, and then discarded it and continued on his way. So he was looking for something, but what? By now I found his actions most puzzling.

At last he seemed to see what he wanted, for he took a few quick strides, bent down, and pulled up what appeared to be a large piece of driftwood half buried in the sand. It must have been about three feet long and as thick as one of the beams in the dining room at Goathlands.

I wondered for what possible reason he could want such an instrument. He examined it quite carefully, took it in both hands, and swung it a couple of times. Then he started to walk purposefully down the beach toward the seal.

I rose to my feet. What on earth could he be doing, I asked myself. He was now walking toward the rock where the seal lay. I began to wonder if perhaps the seal had got stuck and Roger wanted to use the piece of driftwood as a lever in order to free the animal. I held my field glasses to my eyes as Roger approached the seal. He stopped, standing just behind the creature's head, and then, to my horror, he raised the huge piece of wood and brought it crashing down on the poor innocent animal's head.

For a moment I was too stunned and horrified to move, and then as he raised his club for the second time, I dropped my glasses, my hands flew to my face, and I started to stagger toward the cliff edge.

"No! No! No!" I screamed, totally unaware that my steps were taking me closer and closer to that sheer drop of over a hundred feet.

I must have been almost at the cliff edge—another pace would have taken me over and into the void—when strong hands grasped me from behind and flung me to safety.

In my tense and overwrought state, I had been crushed by the sight of Roger's cruelty toward the seal. This was the final straw. I lay where I fell, sobbing hysterically.

"No, no," I moaned through my tears. "Not Roger, dear God, don't let it be him."

Ormerod was kneeling on the grass beside me.

"What is it, Miss Emma? What happened?" There was a catch in his voice as he spoke.

"Let me go, Ormerod," I pleaded. "Please let me go. I've got to get away from here."

"Don't worry, lass," he said. "I'm going to take thee home. This is for wiser heads than mine to sort out. Come on and let me get thee into the motor car."

"I don't want to go home," I cried. "Don't you understand, I can't go home. I haven't got a home."

"I reckon thou's not well, Miss Emma," he said. "I wouldn't want thee to hold this against me, but I'm taking thee home, even if I have to tie thee into the car. Come, lass, I'll help thee in."

In my dazed condition I was quite incapable of any form of resistance. Ormerod picked me up as if I had been no more than a child and deposited me in the passenger seat. As he went to start the motor I made a move to get out.

"Don't try it, Miss Emma. I meant it. I'll tie thee in if thou tries to get away."

I collapsed back into the seat, numbed with the horror of what I had seen. In my mind I saw again the raised club and the ferocious blow as it crushed the life out of one of God's creatures. A man who could do that was capable of anything. That it had to be Roger, Roger whom I believed to be my friend, Roger to whom only an hour ago, I would gladly have given my heart. I tried to think only of the way in which he had rescued me not twenty-four hours before. But had it been a rescue? Might not he have been the one who started that fire, intending not so much to harm my body but rather to terrorize me, to drive me insane?

The doubts and the evil of what surrounded me were too much. I was even beyond tears as I stared blankly at the road ahead while Ormerod drove grimly back to Goathlands.

Chapter Seventeen

I REMEMBER ONLY vaguely our arrival at the house. I sat in the motor car, stunned and stupefied. I remember voices calling to me. Finally someone, I think it was Ormerod, carried me to my room. Then, somehow, I was in bed. Then there was Letty, standing by my bed and holding a glass containing some sort of liquid. She put her arm round my shoulders and raised me to a sitting position. She held the glass to my lips. I think I tried to protest, but the will to fight was no longer in me, and I drank the evil-tasting draught. After that there must have been a period of blessed oblivion, for I remember nothing at all.

How long I lay there, I had no means of knowing. All I did know was that when consciousness returned, I was dimly aware that I was not alone in the room. I opened my eyes and tried to raise my head; it proved to be quite an effort. A woman came to the side of the bed and looked down at me. She was a total stranger.

"Miss Waldron."

"Who are you?" I breathed in reply as she bent over me to catch my words.

"I am Nurse O'Dowd. Dr. Harrison engaged me to look after you.

"I don't want Dr. Harrison," I said.

"Of course you don't," she said appeasingly. "Now, is there anything I can get for you? A little broth perhaps? Do you know you have not eaten for forty-eight hours?"

Forty-eight hours, two days out of my life. What had happened to me? Fear gripped me as I struggled back to consciousness.

"I do not want to see Dr. Harrison," I said again. "Must I see her?"

"Now try and stay calm, Miss Waldron," the nurse said, not answering my question. "You have had a very severe shock. We are not aware of what caused it or what it was, but you became quite hysterical and doctor had to keep you sedated for some little time." She pulled the bell rope by my bed. "And now," she continued, "I think it is time for you to take a little nourishment. You must be very weak, and we want to get your strength back, do we not?"

Letty came in and stood solemnly at the door.

"Ah, Letty," said Nurse. "I should like you to bring Miss Waldron a bowl of beef broth and to inform Dr. Harrison that she is awake."

"Yes, nurse," replied Letty. "Please, Miss Emma, are you feeling better? We've been ever so worried about you."

I nodded to Letty and tried to smile my thanks for her solicitude. She gave me a little smile in reply and went out.

In a few moments she returned with a cup of steaming broth. I sipped it gratefully, and with each mouthful I became more aware of my surroundings and my mind became clearer.

"Please, Nurse," said Letty, turning to her. "Dr. Harrison will be up in a moment."

"Thank you, Letty," replied the nurse. "I think you had better get off to bed now."

Letty smiled at me. "I'll be back this evening, miss," she said.

"What did she mean about coming back this evening?" I asked after Letty had left.

"Letty sits with you during the night," replied Nurse. "She is on duty from nine o'clock in the evening until nine o'clock in the morning when I take over."

I did not reply. The germ of an idea had entered my mind and I wanted time to think about it. I could count on Letty. I had to get away from Goathlands, and through my still befogged mind I was beginning to see a way.

"Is Letty alone with me all night?" I asked.

"That's right," replied the nurse. "Of course, if you need anything or she is worried about anything, she would call either Dr. Harrison or myself."

At that moment Dr. Harrison walked in, and instinctively I shrank from her presence. Even though I told myself that I had nothing to fear from her now, I still found her a very frightening person.

"Well, Miss Waldron," she said in her soft low voice. "I am glad to see you taking a little nourishment. You have been quite ill, and here I must confess that, apart from insuring that you were kept quiet, I have been able to do very little. I can only prescribe rest and nourishment for you. I have asked another doctor to come over from York and have a look at you. He will be arriving this afternoon and will come up for a little chat. In the meantime, I would like you to continue to rest. Sleep if you can, and if you want anything in the way of food, do not hesitate to ask for it." She turned to the nurse. "I think we had better just leave her until Doctor Wilson has had a chance to make his own diagnosis."

Dr. Harrison nodded to the nurse, who followed her out into my sitting room. I could hear their voices, low in conversation. I must confess that I strained to hear what they were saying but was unable to make out the words.

The details of my plan were beginning to form in my mind. Since one of the things I would want was all the knowledge I could muster, I would have no hesitation about eavesdropping whenever the opportunity arose. I wanted to discuss the whole thing with Letty. If Letty was to have sole charge of me through the night, I should be able to use that time to attain my objective. Letty was the only one of whose loyalty I was certain. If I was going to do this, I would need to get all the rest I could get during the day in order to be fresh at night when she was on duty.

Nurse came back into the bedroom carrying a bunch of roses.

"Here's a present for you, Miss Waldron," she said.

"How lovely." I smiled. "Whom are they from?"

"There's a card, I'll read it to you," she replied. " 'Get well soon, please may I call on you,' and it is signed 'Roger.' "

Roger! What was he up to now? Gloating over the fact that he had succeeded? Oh, how foolish one can be. I wanted so much to take the flowers and press them to my bosom, but even as I looked at them, I saw again the raised club, the figure diving through the smoke, the only person within a mile of that fire. The roses became repulsive in my sight.

"Put them in the other room, Nurse," I said. "I do not want to see anyone. I would rather not be disturbed, if you can arrange that. And now, if you don't mind, I should like to sleep."

"Very good, Miss Waldron," she replied. "I shall be in the sitting room. There is a handbell by your bed. If you want me, just ring."

She left, and I lay back on my pillows and tried to relax.

I must have slept very soundly, for the next thing I was aware of was Nurse bending over me saying that she was sorry to disturb me, but the doctor had arrived.

A tall, gray-haired, distinguished-looking man was standing at the foot of the bed. This, I presumed, must be Dr. Wilson. Dr. Harrison was standing at his side, and both of them were looking at me intently.

"Now then," he said. "Perhaps you would like to tell me all about it."

"All about what?" I demanded.

"You have been through a great emotional strain, and we are trying to find out why."

"I don't want to discuss anything," I replied. "I am very tired and I want to go to sleep."

"Come, come, Miss Waldron," he said. "Just answer one or two questions and I shall be glad to leave you alone. Supposing you start by telling me about your teddy bear. Where is it, by the way?"

That beastly teddy bear again. Suddenly I began to realize what was happening. The suave professional manner, the questions couched in almost childish terms; they thought I was mad. Well, even if that was so, I had no intention of assisting them in their task.

"I am certainly not going to talk about anything so childish as teddy bears," I snapped. "Will you please all go away and leave me alone. I don't think that either of you have any right to treat me against my will."

The doctors glanced at each other.

"I think it might be better if we retired to the other room and discussed the whole question with Sir Joshua," said Dr. Wilson.

So Uncle Josh was here as well. I sat up in my bed biting my lip, waiting to see what they would do.

"Just as you say, doctor," replied Dr. Harrison. "Nurse."

The three of them trooped out, closing the door behind

them. In a flash I was out of the bed and had my ear glued
to the door. I could only make out snatches of their conversation, but I managed to get the gist of what they were
saying. Dr. Wilson seemed all for removing me from
Goathlands and into his "clinic," as he called it, though I
got the feeling that his so-called clinic was likely to prove
to be some sort of asylum. Uncle Joshua seemed to object
to this, saying things such as, "It is much too early to
make such a decision." I was unable to decipher anything
that Dr. Harrison said; her soft voice was too low to pene-
trate the thick oaken panels of the door.

Uncle Joshua said, "I am going to have a word with her
alone, and I don't want to be interrupted."

As he spoke I rushed back to my bed and was just pulling up the blankets when the door opened and Uncle Josh
came in. I looked at him intently, though it was impossible
to make an estimate of his feelings; his poor face was quite
incapable of expressing any emotion.

"Hello, Emma," he said.

"Hello, uncle," I replied. And then I said, "They all
think I am mad, don't they?"

"Of course not, my dear. We do feel that you are a little
overwrought and in some small way in need of medical attention." He paused, but as I did not offer any comment,
he continued. "Dr. Wilson feels that it would be a good idea
if you were to spend a period in his hospital. Dr. Harrison
is not so sure. She feels that with constant supervision you
would soon be your old self again. I, for my part, have
told him that I shall consent to nothing until I have discussed the matter with you and given you time to make up
your own mind. What do you say?"

"Uncle," I replied. "I only want to go back to London."

"I am sorry, but that is out of the question at the moment. I should never forgive myself if anything were to
happen to you and I had let you out of my care. I'll tell

you what we shall do. Let us give it a couple of days before coming to a decision. A great deal may change in that time. Meanwhile, just you get as much rest as you can and we'll talk about it the day after tomorrow."

Uncle Joshua left me, and I heard the sounds of departure coming from my sitting room. I realized that my plan to escape from Goathlands now had to be completed and executed within forty-eight hours. I was not prepared to risk waiting for my next meeting with Uncle Joshua; that might be too late. Nurse came into my room.

"Is there anything I can get you, Miss Waldron?" she asked.

"I should like you to bring a clock in here," I replied. "You will find one on the mantlepiece in the sitting room, that will do unless you have need of it in there."

She seemed very surprised at my request but complied nonetheless. The reason that I had asked for a clock was that timing was essential to my plan and there was no clock in the bedroom. Nurse brought in the clock and wanted to know if there was anything else that she could do for me. I told her that I was tired and intended to sleep, so she left me alone after again insuring that the hand bell was within easy reach. My fatigue was quite genuine. The effects of the sedative they had been giving me were still apparent, and it was not long before I once more fell asleep.

When I awoke it was pitch dark and very still. I could not see the clock, though I could hear it ticking away. I reached out cautiously for the bell and rang. The door opened and a figure carrying a candle entered. It was Letty.

"Are you all right, miss?" she whispered. "Did you want something?"

"I'm perfectly all right, Letty," I replied. "Will you tell me what time it is?"

"I don't know, miss, the clock's gone." With an echo of the old frightened Letty that I had first met, she added, "I didn't move it, miss."

"I know you didn't, Letty, it's over there." I pointed in the general direction of clock.

"It's half past two, miss."

"Good!" I replied.

Half past two would suit my purpose admirably. The household would be quiet and there would be very little likelihood of any interruption. I got out of bed.

"Where are you going, Miss Emma?" asked Letty.

"I am going to sit down in the sitting room and have a long talk with you," I replied.

"But, miss, I'm supposed to call Nurse or Dr. Harrison if you get up."

Here was a snag. I had to convince her that that was the one thing that she must not do.

"Letty," I said. "I trust you. I sincerely believe that you are my friend, possibly the only friend I have in this house. Now, more than anything, I need your trust in me. I want to talk to you, but I don't want to have to explain too much. It would take too long, and if you knew everything it might prove dangerous. So I am asking you now, will you trust me and help me?"

"Of course I'll help you, miss, I'll do anything for you, but. . . ."

"No buts, Letty. In asking you to help I am putting myself completely at your mercy, but I must have help and you are the only one to whom I can turn." I waited to allow my remarks to sink in. She seemed to be thinking it over, and then quite suddenly, she made her decision.

"I'll do anything you ask, miss."

"And not ask questions?"

"I'll try not to, miss."

It was difficult to express in words the gratitude I felt

toward this small, waiflike creature, so I said, quite simply, "Thank you, Letty, I will make sure that you never regret taking this decision. Now, see if you can find my dressing gown."

She produced the dressing gown and we went through into the sitting room. I was still feeling quite weak and knew that the first thing I needed was food.

"Letty," I said, "can you get me something to eat?"

"I suppose so, miss," she replied. "But if Mrs. Jollyman ever finds out—" She did not dwell on the horrifying thought of Mrs. Jollyman's wrath.

"Never mind about Mrs. Jollyman," I said. "Run down to the kitchen and get hold of whatever you can find and a pot of hot coffee if you can manage it."

"I'll do it, miss," she said, suddenly becoming quite conspiratorial. She slipped out of the room in such a stealthy manner that under different circumstances I should have burst out laughing.

While she was out of the room, I went back into the bedroom and scribbled my London address on a piece of paper and got five gold sovereigns out of my purse.

It was not more than ten minutes before she returned, carrying a tray piled with hot soup, half a cold pheasant, and a pot of coffee.

"Here you are, miss. I hope it's enough."

It was enough to feed a regiment. I suggested that she pull up a chair and share it with me, but somehow the idea seemed to shock her. However, she did consent to drink a cup of coffee. This she drank from my toothbrush mug as she had only brought one cup with her. I had a good meal and ate mostly in silence while Letty sat uncomfortably on the edge of the armchair facing me and drank her coffee. At length, I finished and poured out my own coffee.

"Now, Letty," I said. "We had better get down to business. I have to get away from Goathlands. I do not want to appear melodramatic, but I have very good reasons for believing that there is someone in this house who is trying to cause me grievous harm."

"But why would anyone want to harm you, miss?"

"Why indeed?" I replied. "But no questions. The others would, for the best possible reasons, try to prevent my leaving. I cannot, I must not, go into details. Suffice it to say that it is imperative that I get away. I have a plan, and in order to carry it out I must have the help which you have promised me. First let me tell you what I intend doing. I shall leave here before eight o'clock this morning and catch the ten o'clock train from Malton to York, from where I shall be able to get a connection to London. I would take you with me, but I need you to remain here in order to keep everyone unaware of my departure for as long as possible.

"As soon as they discover your part in this, I am fairly certain that you will be discharged. When this happens, I should like you to come straight to this address in London." I handed her the paper on which I had written my address. "No, don't say anything yet. You will need money, so here are five sovereigns. I am sure that will be sufficient until you and I meet again. We can discuss your future then, but I promise that I shall see that you are well provided for."

"But, miss, how are you going to get to Malton?" asked Letty.

"Ah," I replied. "That is where I must have your help. I intend to ride to Malton. It is just over eighteen miles, and if I can get away from here before eight I shall be there in time to catch the train. What I want you to do is to have Honey saddled and ready to leave by a quarter to eight. Ormerod and the grooms will be starting work at eight o'clock, so if I can leave then I should be out of sight before they arrive. That's it, Letty, will you do it?"

"Of course I'll do it, Miss Emma, but. . . ."

"But what, Letty?"

"I haven't ever touched a horse, miss, I wouldn't know where to start."

Poor Letty, she looked utterly crestfallen. This was indeed a serious blow to my plan. What on earth could I do now? Willing though she was, it would be hopeless to let her try. I could try and do it myself, but I would need what little strength I had for the two hour ride to Malton. Besides, I did not want to expose myself until it was absolutely necessary. I came to a decision. I had to take a chance and look for extra help. For obvious reasons, it could not be Roger, and Doctor Harrison was out of the question. In any case, Henry was the one person whom I had never really suspected.

"Letty," I said, "is Mr. Henry at home?"

"Oh yes, miss," she replied. "He was in the big barn all day talking to Mr. Attwood and messing about with the flying machine."

"Do you know where his room is?" She nodded in reply. "Go and wake him up and bring him here."

Letty returned in a couple of minutes.

"He was very surprised, miss, but he's coming," she said.

A few moments later Henry walked in.

"I must say, it's a strange hour to ask a gentleman to call, coz," he said, with his usual mocking smile. "Are you feeling better and want a chat?"

"Henry," I said, "please be serious. I need help. I want you to listen to what I have to say and then please help me."

"Sorry, coz," he said. "If there's anything I can do, you only have to ask."

He and Letty sat in silence while I told them the whole story. I told them about the teddy bear, the burnt papers, the cut girth, the fire, and finally I told them about the seal.

"The swine," murmured Henry when I recounted this last incident. "Just wait till I get my hands on him."

I begged Henry to take no action against Roger and then went on to tell him about my plan to escape.

"Well," I concluded, "what do you think?"

He paused for quite a long time before replying. I could tell that he was thinking hard, so Letty and I sat in silence, waiting for him to speak.

"It's a good idea, you must get away from here until we can get this business sorted out," he began. "But as far as your plan is concerned, I'm going to suggest a few alterations, because as it stands you're sure to be spotted before you are out of the grounds. First, you must not take Honey; that would be too obvious. You must take my mare. Can you ride astride?"

"I never have done," I replied.

"That will be tricky, but we can manage. Now, here's what we'll do. I shall go down to the stables now and put a side saddle into the summer house. You be there at half past seven. I shall get my mare, tack her up, and ride her round to the summer house. If anybody sees anything they'll just think that I am going for a ride before breakfast. It will probably surprise them, but it won't arouse suspicion. When I get to the summer house, we'll switch saddles and you can be on your way. What do you think?"

I thought it was a splendid idea, much better than my original, and I told Henry so. I tried to thank him, but he would hear none of it. He asked Letty to keep everyone out of my bedroom for as long as possible so that I could have the maximum amount of time to get on my way before the inevitable hue and cry. He then wisely suggested that I rest until it was time to move. He went to the door, turned, and said, "See you in the summer house, coz."

Chapter Eighteen

THE SUMMER HOUSE stands about a quarter of a mile from the main building on top of a little grassy mound. It is surrounded on three sides by trees, leaving the fourth side open to the south, overlooking Howl Moor and Pickering Forest beyond. From the summer house it was possible to see both the main house and the big barn, though you could not see the stables as these were obscured by the big barn. The advantage, from my point of view, was that while it was possible to see through the trees anything that happened in the area around the house, it was almost impossible to see the summer house except from the south side.

My route to Malton would take me over Howl Moor and across Blawath Beck, near the point where I had had my fall. From there, I intended to cut through a corner of Pickering Forest. This would bring me out onto Levisham Moor. Levisham Moor was almost seven miles across, and it was mostly rocky scrub, which I would have to take at a fairly slow pace. However, once across the Pickering to Scarborough road, which skirted the moor on its south side, I would be in flat open country and able to ride fast for the remainder of my journey into Malton.

I felt that the first couple of miles would be the most dangerous. After the first hundred yards or so, I would be riding in easy view of the house until I crossed Blawath Beck and got into the forest. But for the remainder of my journey, I should be safe from observation.

For the first time, Letty helped me to dress. She wisely

insisted that I wear a heavy tweed coat over my riding
habit, as it was likely to be quite chilly once I got outside.
There was also another reason: the long coat would help
me to look less incongruous once I boarded my train. People did not usually travel to London dressed for riding. I
made sure that I had sufficient money in my purse, and
well before seven-thirty, after a rather sad farewell from
Letty, I was on my way out of the house and hurrying toward the summer house. I did not look back before I got
there. The door was open, and I found my saddle inside. I
looked this over carefully, remembering the cut girth, but
found that everything was in order. I was glad of my coat,
for the little building was cold on that fresh October morning. But the weather looked set fair, and the prospect of a
pleasant day and an easy ride seemed to buoy up my
spirits.

Looking back toward the main buildings, I saw, to my
surprise, that Kittiwake had been rolled out in front of the
big barn. Perhaps Roger was going to fly her today.
Thinking of Roger brought a pang of regret as I tried to
imagine what might have been. I had never been so close
to happiness, and at the same time it had never been so
difficult to grasp. There was Uncle Josh, too; what was I
doing to him? For a moment I wavered in my purpose, but
only for a moment, for by then I could see Henry. He was
already rounding the big barn, mounted on his big black
mare. What a fine figure my cousin cut, sitting hard down
in his saddle, his back straight as a ramrod. He rode his
horse like a cavalry officer, though I knew he had never
had any leanings toward the military life.

Henry urged the animal into a trot and passed by the
summer house at some little distance. For a moment I was
fearful lest he was about to ride off and leave me there,
but soon I realized that he was waiting until the summer
house obscured him from the main buildings before turning and approaching from the south.

Within a very few minutes he was with me.

"Well done, coz," he said, dismounting and unbuckling his girth. "Did anybody see you?"

"I don't think so," I replied.

"That's good. Now we must waste no time. Get me your saddle."

By this time he had removed his saddle, and I handed him mine, which he immediately threw across the horse's back. He buckled the girth and gave the straps a final heave.

"There," he said. "You'll be all right now. I've put a pelham on her; she's a bit fresh, but you'll be able to hold her with that. Now, are you all right for money?"

"Oh yes, I have plenty," I replied.

"I wish I could say the same," he answered. "Now, when you get to Malton, you can leave the horse with one of the cab drivers. Tell him that I shall collect her later today and I'll give him a half sovereign if he gives her a decent feed and a rubdown."

The question of what to do with the horse was something else I had not thought of. I thought, what a good thing I had taken Henry into my confidence, he was certainly proving a worthy ally.

At last he seemed satisfied, and everything was ready. He looked at me, smiling that strange twisted smile of his.

"Here, you had better take this." He handed me his riding crop. "And now, we're ready for off."

He gave me a leg up into the saddle. I leaned over and kissed him lightly.

"I don't know how long it will be before you can come back to Goathlands," he said. "I've got a lot of investigating to do. I'll write you as soon as I am sure it is safe."

I started to say something, but he interrupted me.

"No speeches. No farewells. No thanks. On your way, and good luck."

He slapped the horse on the rump, and I was off.

I headed south across Howl Moor, and within ten minutes or so I was approaching Blawath Beck. The mare jumped it easily and lightly, though when she landed on the other side, she was pulling hard and fighting for her head. Henry had been right; she really was quite fresh. I was glad of the additional control that the curb chain on the pelham gave me, for it would have been foolish to let her have her head then with such a long ride in front of us. Apart from any other consideration, it would have been dangerous to go too fast through the forest. The animal's speed would be put to much better use when I got to the open meadow below Levisham Moor.

Moments after crossing the beck, we were in amongst the trees. These were beginning to lose their leaves, and the heaviest of the summer vegetation was fast disappearing from underfoot, so I was able to take a fairly direct path through the wood. I covered the mile or so between Blawath Beck and Levisham Moor in very good time.

I had assumed that it would take me half an hour or so to get to the edge of the moor, and we did, in fact, get there in well under that. As we emerged from the wood we encountered a small stream, which the mare jumped easily. Then we set off at an extended trot up the hill and toward the top of the moor.

As we breasted the top of the hill, I stopped my mount and looked back toward the north. The point at which we had now arrived was situated about five miles from Goathlands and overlooked Pickering Forest in the valley below. The house was still just visible as a small blob on the horizon. I wondered if I would ever look upon it again.

The air was very still; in the quiet of that autumn morning, it would have been possible to hear a bird singing a mile away. Was it my imagination, I wondered, or did I hear the sound of a motor coming from the direction of Goathlands? For a moment my heart missed a beat as I hought that my absence might have been noticed already. But no, that was not possible, for it was not yet nine o'clock. The first person to realize that I was missing would surely be the nurse, and she did not come on duty until nine. It was then that I remembered seeing Kittiwake by the big barn. Perhaps, even at this very moment, Roger was taking the flying machine up into the air. If he was, I wished him well. In spite of everything, in spite of my fear of him, I could not find it in my nature to wish him ill.

There was no point in standing there thinking of what might have been. I turned the mare south and started off down the hill and toward the main road, now about five miles distant.

One had to take care crossing this part of the moor, as the surface was very broken and abounded with stones and rocks, some of which were as large as small boulders.

Again, I heard the sound of a motor, and this time there could be no doubt about it. I looked back over my shoulder. There, its silver wings glinting in the sunlight, coming high over the top of the hill I was descending, was Kittiwake. A lump came to my throat as I looked at this strange and beautiful machine and thought of Roger, whom I would never see again. I could just make out the black-coated, helmeted figure sitting in the cockpit as the machine banked away past me in a gentle arc.

As the mare picked her way through the stones and rocks, I watched the flying machine with the hunched figure sitting at the controls as it winged away from me. I wondered whether he had noticed me and if he had, what emotion had stirred within him.

When Kittiwake was about half a mile past me, it turned a half circle. I supposed that he was now returning to Goathlands. He was flying in my direction and seemed to be getting lower all the time. Nearer and nearer he came, until I could see the masked face through the whirl-

ing disc of the propeller. I felt the mare shiver beneath me;
she had seen the flying machine, and I could feel that she
was worried. Suddenly, I realized to my horror that the
machine was flying straight at me. Closer and closer it
came. I was frozen with terror. Just as it seemed that it
was inevitable that it should fly right into me, it zoomed
upwards, clearing me by no more than a few feet.

The mare reared and bucked, which was hardly surprising. I had to fight to bring her under control. I had no wish
to be thrown onto the rocks over which we were passing.

I glanced over my shoulder. The machine was making
another turn. It swung away to the right and then round in
a half circle and straight toward us again. This was not a
game; he was trying to kill me. Like a hunted animal, I
searched around for a way of escape. If only I could reach
the forest. But that was over a mile away.

The machine was upon us again. As it roared over my
head, I could almost have touched it. The mare shied violently, and suddenly she bolted. Now I was in real trouble.
I pulled on her head with all my strength, but it was no
use. She had taken the bit between her teeth and was rushing over the rough, dangerous ground in a blind panic.

"Stop! Stop! Stop!" I screamed aloud.

ZOOOOOOOM. The flying machine with that devil at
the controls tore across in front of us. The mare swerved
violently. I lost a stirrup. I was now clinging on for dear
life. The reins had gone and I was clutching frantically at
the animal's mane, but now she was heading straight for
the forest. If only I could stay on. If only she did not turn.
In her panic she was stumbling at every other step, but she
was still heading toward the trees.

I could not see the flying machine, but in a moment I
heard the roar of its engine. It was behind me. Now I was
urging the mare on. The trees were getting closer and
closer. The noise of the machine was getting louder and
louder. Suddenly it was on top of us, the wheels seemed to

e inches above my head, and then he was past and there
as a shattering explosion.

In a split second the mare stopped and I was thrown
ut of the saddle.

I scrambled to my feet, not caring about my cuts and
ruises. There in front of me was a blazing inferno that
ad only seconds before been a man and a machine. So in-
ent had he been on his fiendish purpose that he must not
ave seen the tall trees just ahead, and he had flown
traight into them.

I staggered over the stones toward the wreckage, for
hat purpose I know not. Any possibility of rescue was
ut of the question. I think I was aware of the beat of gal-
oping hooves as I scrambled toward the little stream
eyond which lay the blazing mass that held all that was
eft of my tormentor.

I stood at the edge of the stream, sobbing aloud, the
ears streaming down my cheeks.

"Oh, Roger, Roger," I cried. "Didn't you know that I
oved you? Didn't you know that I would gladly have
iven you all that a woman has to offer? Oh, my love, oh,
ny darling, why did it have to be you, why did it have to
e you? Oh, Roger, I loved you so very very much."

"Would you mind saying that again?"

I knew that it couldn't be. I knew that I was mad and
hat my imagination was playing me tricks and that soon
hey would shut me away with other poor demented souls
o eke out my fantasy existence.

"I said, would you mind repeating that?"

A wave of hope welled up within me, and yet I hardly
ared to turn, fearful lest the illusion should vanish. Slow-
y I forced my body round. I looked, I saw. It was he.

"Roger," I whispered.

He stepped very close to me and placed his hands on my
houlders.

"Emma, Emma my beloved, thank God you're safe."

He gazed deep into my tear-filled eyes. "Did you mean it" Can it really be true? Look at me and tell me that it i true."

I looked into his blue-gray eyes, now all serious witl hope and longing. I knew that it was true; I knew tha even if it had been him at the controls of that machine, i would still be true. I knew that whatever he was, whateve: he did, he was my man and I would willingly follow him to the ends of the earth.

"Roger," I said. "Look at me and you will know that i is true. No woman can look upon a man as I look upo you now without love."

In that instant, I was in his arms and sobbing my hear out.

"Don't cry, my darling. Everything is all right now Look, the fire is almost out. It's finished, it's over. I'n going to take you home."

I looked over to the wreckage. There Ormerod and A1 thur were beating out the last of the flames. My mare an three other horses were drinking peacefully from th stream. Roger led me to the mare and lifted me into th saddle. He mounted his horse and together we turned ou: mounts north and headed toward Goathlands.

Chapter Nineteen

IT IS JANUARY in the year nineteen hundred and twenty My husband and I are in London, and at this moment w are standing in the entrance lobby of Brown's Hotel i1 Dover Street, having arrived from Yorkshire last night More than ten years have now passed since that terribl day when I stood watching the fire raging on the edge of Pickering Forest.

It was Henry, of course, who died that day. Poor Henry who was so much a product of his generation. Born into a comfortable, wealthy home where he had never had the desire nor the urging to do anything with his life, confident that the family coffers were a bottomless pit and that the British Empire would stand and protect him forever.

It had been Henry all the time. Over the years I have often wondered what my cousin felt toward me. I like to feel that it was not hatred, but that in his selfish, indolent mind he had merely regarded me as a means to an end.

We had discovered, though it took many months for all of the facts to come to light, that he was so deeply in debt that, unless he was to spend the rest of his days being hounded by creditors, it was absolutely necessary for him to get his hands onto my share of my grandfather's fortune.

That he was a gambler and had lost money was known to most people, but the massive extent of his debts was beyond anyone's imagination. The incident which I had observed that Sunday outside the church had been one of many. A small matter of ten pounds owed to a local bookmaker. So desperate were his finances that he was incapable of raising even that comparatively small sum.

I found out that Uncle Joshua had long since stopped helping him out of his monetary difficulties, and it appeared that he had then started borrowing from moneylenders on the strength of his expected inheritance.

When I arrived at Goathlands, his entire expectation had been mortgaged up to the hilt, and the sum was growing daily larger as the exorbitant interest charges mounted up. His one hope of getting himself out of the mess he was in was to gain control of my share of our grandfather's fortune.

According to grandfather's will, should either of us die or become incapable of administering our inheritance, the whole sum was to pass to the other. Henry had two choices: either he could drive me insane or he could kill me.

I suppose, and this can only be conjecture, that his first intention was to drive me mad. However, I committed a near fatal error when, that night, I decided to take him into my confidence regarding my intention to escape from Goathlands. The one thing he could not allow to happen was for me to leave Goathlands, so that I would no longer be in his power. He must have been desperate. I still shudder when I think back and remember how he sat there in my sitting room, sympathizing with me, helping me to plan my escape, and all the time plotting my doom.

Poor Henry. During our ride back to the house after the crash, Roger told me that Ormerod had seen Kittiwake take off. Ormerod had asked Roger whether Mr. Henry knew how to handle the machine. Roger, Ormerod, and Arthur had immediately ridden off, following the flight of Kittiwake without any knowledge of my plight. They had feared that Henry might damage the machine and possibly injure himself. I could imagine their horror as they got to the top of Levisham Moor and saw the machine swooping down upon me. The first time it happened, they thought, as I did myself, that Henry was just being stupid and showing off. But when it happened twice more, Roger recognized that I was in deadly danger and spurred his horse in my direction, yelling to the others to try and keep Kittiwake in sight as he did so.

If only Henry had come to me, if only he had told me the desperate trouble he was in. I would have helped him; I could have done no less. But he did not and as a result died horribly.

The hall porter comes over to my husband and says

something to him in a low voice. My husband is turning to me.

"The taxicab is here."

Now he leads me out of the hotel, and there is the commissionaire holding open the door of the taxi. My husband helps me in, and now he is sitting down beside me.

We were married the following spring at the little church in Goathland Village. The Reverend Cox performed the ceremony, and dear Ormerod gave me away. It was too much to ask Uncle Josh to do. He had been in a state of near collapse in those months following the crash. Shortly after our wedding, he died. His end was merciful —he went to bed one night and never woke up. Uncle Joshua had never recovered from the shock of finding out about his son. We had all tried to keep as much as possible from him, but what we did not tell him I am sure he guessed. The tragedy seemed to kill all of his great spirit. He never tried to interest himself in anything else during the few short months that remained him. Even when Roger started to construct a second Kittiwake, he could raise no enthusiasm in Uncle Josh. His attitude toward me was one of constant self-reproach. I think he felt responsible for all the troubles which I had had.

The taxicab is turning out of Dover Street and into the rush of traffic that is Piccadilly. As the cab swings to the right, I am fingering the brooch at my throat. As always, when I touch it my hand steals into that of my husband.

The brooch is made of white gold and has two rubies for eyes; it is in the form of a seal. Whenever I touch it I remind myself never again to make a judgment at first sight.

That day at Robin Hood's Bay, Roger brought his coble round from Whitby, and as he beached the craft, he noticed the young seal on the rocks quite near him. As there was no sign of either myself or Ormerod on the beach, he walked toward the animal, wondering how close he would get before it slid into the sea. He thought how strange it was when the creature did not move, and his interest became more intense the nearer he got to the seal. When he got within touching distance and the seal still did not move, he finally saw the reason. The seal had been most horribly mauled, probably by a shark. The poor creature was in agony, and as Roger had no gun with him, he did the only other thing possible to end the beast's suffering. The massive blow I saw him strike was not the act of cruelty which it appeared to be, but an act of mercy. My jumping to conclusions on that occasion was to teach me a lesson I would never forget.

We are driving past the Ritz Hotel, beyond which lies Green Park. At the end of Piccadilly I can see Hyde Park Corner and St. George's Hospital. It is strange to think that Doctor Susan Harrison is probably even now within those gray walls.

I never got to know Doctor Harrison. I don't suppose we exchanged a couple of hundred words in all the time we were at Goathlands together. Three times only did I see her show any sort of emotion. The first was on the occasion when she ordered me out of Uncle Joshua's room. The second was when she heard about Henry and she expressed her sorrow at having added, innocently though it was, to my sufferings. The last occasion was when Uncle Joshua died. She wept. I often wondered if, in her own strange way, she had been in love with my uncle. Certainly the care and devotion which she lavished on him during his last few days, the sleepless nights which she spent by his bedside, went far beyond the call of duty. It may have been that that cold exterior was merely a facade and be-

ind it lay a passionate desire to relieve suffering wherever
might be found.

Uncle Joshua showed his gratitude by leaving her a sub-
tantial sum in his will, which she used to set up a medical
esearch project.

She left Goathlands a few days after my uncle's death,
nd I have never seen her again. However, I have always
nown where she is, for every Christmas we exchange
ards.

I look up at the hospital as we swing left into Constitu-
ion Hill and wonder if she is still wearing her black dress
nd my aunt's cameo brooch.

My husband is pulling out his watch and glancing at it
nxiously. I give his hand a little squeeze. There is no need
o worry, we are in plenty of time, but I know that he must
e nervous so I smile at him and try to give him a little
confidence.

"The children will be so proud of you today," I whis-
er.

He smiles back at me. I see that he is still uneasy and I
augh quietly to myself.

Within the first three and a half years of our marriage,
we were blessed with two beautiful children. The first was
a boy, Justin, who is now eight, and next came our daugh-
er, Deborah. Debby is nearly seven and dotes on her
brother, following him around everywhere and watching
im with wide-eyed wonder whatever he might be doing.

I think that Justin is going to be a carpenter. A few days
go he presented us with a table he made from odd scraps
of wood. Only three of the legs would touch the ground at
he same time, but nevertheless we had to have our tea
rom it, at Deborah's insistence.

We left Goathlands yesterday, and this is the first time
in the children's short lives that I have been separated

from them for more than a few hours. I feared that they might worry but, oh dear me no, they looked forward with conspiratorial relish to the prospect of being alone with Aunt Letty for a few days.

Dear Letty. I find it difficult even now to realize that the nervous waif whom I met on my first morning at Goathlands turned into a tower of strength within a fortnight.

Shortly after Uncle Joshua's death, she married her Arthur, and I did not see much of her for the next few years. We gave her a cottage and about thirty acres as a wedding present, and she seemed to be settling down there very happily. Then came the war. Arthur, like so many of the young men of his generation, enlisted immediately.

It was a morning in the spring of nineteen fifteen that I returned to my sitting room, where I found Letty weeping quietly. She did not speak but handed me a buff piece of paper. I did not even need to read it, for I knew what it contained.

The War Office regrets to inform you that. . . .

Letty came back into the house. We persuaded her to sell her little farm and invest the money. I am not sure what would be the correct term to describe her present position in the house. I don't believe in nannies for the children, but Letty is more than a nanny to Justin and Debby. We have never had a housekeeper, but Letty is more than a housekeeper. I suppose that she is just Letty.

We are swinging around Victoria Memorial at the bottom of Constitution Hill and pausing at the gates of Buckingham Palace while our driver gives a word of explanation to the policeman on duty there. My poor husband is tight-lipped and gripping my hand fiercely. I think he must imagine that they are going to chop his head off.

Ormerod has retired to his little cottage, where he holds daily court to our children, telling them all the secrets of moor and woodland, sea and shore. I am sure that our youngsters are much more knowledgeable about nature than either of us ever were. Should we ever be bold enough to venture an opinion, we are almost certain to be answered with . . .

"But Uncle Ormerod says. . . ."

Funny thing, to this day I still don't know his first name. I sometimes wonder if he has one.

We are through the big central arch and into the inner courtyard. A footman, magnificent in purple, opens the door of the taxi. We alight and are ushered into a large anteroom in which are a number of other people, mostly serving men in their uniforms.

Roger tried very hard to get into one or another of the fighting services, but his knowledge of flying machines was such that his country would not allow him to go to war. He spent those four terrible years researching and building aeroplanes. His impressive record in this field is, in fact, the reason for our presence here today.

We are waiting. It is not for long, but I can see from the expression on my husband's face that he feels that it is an eternity.

At last a servant in evening dress calls us, and we are escorted into the throne room. A minute passes and my husband's name is called.

He approaches a small man with a beard, dressed in the uniform of Admiral of the Fleet.

A word or two pass between them, and then my husband kneels.

George the Fifth, by the Grace of God, King of Britain and Her Dominions Beyond the Seas, Defender of the

Faith, Emperor of India, takes a sword from an equerry and taps my husband on the shoulder. The King speaks.

"Arise, Sir Roger Attwood."